Adam

'I think it splendid. This book does successfully a
very difficult thing. To have a sensuous imagination,
at once robust and delicate, is much. To embody it
in words is more. To do this continually without
cloying and suffocating the reader — to combine
such richness with such freshness — is more still. But
to re-tell the story of Adam as Mr Bolt has done is
most of all. There is no patronage, no parody, no
allegorization. The book seems to rise of itself out of
prolonged meditation; the author has seen it taking
just this shape. We with him, feel it would not have
been otherwise. A false step would have been fatal,
but the author makes none.'
C. S. Lewis

'It has so moved me that I find it impossible to put
into words what I feel about it . . . it is a true work of
inspiration, a slow welling up of power and beauty. It
leaves the reader thankful to have read it.'
Elizabeth Goudge

'It is extremely effective and should appeal to those
who like fine, imaginative writing . . .'
Publisher's Weekly

David Bolt was born in Middlesex, England, and
educated at Dulwich College. After serving in the
Indian Army and the Malayan Police, he entered
bookselling and became a buyer in Durban, South
Africa. His first novel, *The Albatross*, appeared in
1954. It was followed by further novels and a short
work on theology, *Of Heaven and Hope*.

ADAM

David Bolt

A LION PAPERBACK

Copyright © 1960 David Bolt

Published by
Lion Publishing
Icknield Way, Tring, Herts, England
ISBN 0 85648 372 9
Albatross Books
PO Box 320, Sutherland, NSW 2232, Australia
ISBN 0 86760 334 8

First edition 1960 J. M. Dent
First paperback edition 1981
Published by arrangement with
Sidgwick and Jackson Ltd

Printed and bound in Great Britain by Richard Clay
(The Chaucer Press) Ltd, Bungay, Suffolk

For Jane Eve

O that there were such an heart in them, that they would fear me, and keep all my commandments always, that it might be well with them, and with their children for ever!

DEUTERONOMY 5 : 29.

Contents

❖❖❖❖❖❖❖❖❖❖❖❖❖❖❖❖❖❖❖❖❖❖❖❖

The Dragon

THE PEAK on which he stood was already lichened over with a greenness: and yet so finely that the least flexing of his talons scraped white. He stood on three legs nursing a fourth lame, with his wings folded back, watching.

About and above him curved the blue depths of the firmament itself, enflamed with a golden and burning glory. The brightness of it hooded his eyes. Horizon to horizon below lay seas of sand in a glittering stillness, silver-white to the ends of the earth; dunefalls like ocean waves fading far away into the rippling distance: and yet motionless.

Between *wána* and *wéna*, earth and sky, was no breath of wind or life.

Down there nothing moved. Only the shadows diminishing, little by little, withdrew gradually smaller and smaller under the dunes.

When the sun reached its highest point a heat haze formed on the face of the earth. In the silence he could measure his own heart's ache, and the resentful throbbing under his ribs. He shifted his lame foot a little.

East to West suddenly a new shadow, blurred with the haze and its own swiftness, small and winged—he jerked his head up, onyx eyes slanting to find the cause of it. But the sun blinded him. It was a moment before he found the shadow again, immediately below as it passed, traversing the sandfields, switchbacking the contours of the dunes: and then it was gone.

He moved at last, stretching himself out, arching the scaled length of his spine. Then he turned quickly.

On the rock edge there rested, echo of flight, a single feather of a cool sea-blue, shading to sea-green at the tip. For a moment it trembled and then, wafted with the little breeze of its own falling, drifted over the lip and vanished from sight.

Before he left the peak he lifted his head in one long last challenging glance upwards, proud to the familiar heavens, unclasping the strength of his wings as though, for an instant, he would spread them: then abruptly turned in one quickening movement, rapidly following his shadow close down over the green rock slope.

The descent was more difficult than he had expected. Among the clefts his lame foot troubled him, so that he was obliged to use his long and powerful tail for balance, flinging it side to side, coming down in a slithering that bruised the softer scales of his underbelly. Twice he thrust and clawed to secure a hold, slithered, and held fast in pain. His breath, torn from him in gusts, seared his nostrils wide. He stood in a fury of tears until the hurt of it abated, and began cautiously downwards again.

How long it took him, he could not afterwards tell.

The sun in its course followed him down, and darkness overtook him; and overhead stars came through one by one, Orion, and Arcturus, and the Pleiades—he could name them all. He made his way down by moonlight, the crescent moon high over the black mass of rock above him, clear and bright and afterwards waning again to give way to the first rising of the sun: the low skies streaked with crimson flames whitening to the full blaze of glory.

When the sun was on high, looking down he saw the haze over the sandfields a long fall below him still.

But now through the nearer haze the ring of horizons quivered in a rising vapour, losing distinctness. White merged into blue, blue to a silvery whiteness, blending and fusing into one. He came down through veil after veil of haze in a half-light: the burning brightness diffused, cooling to a translucence, filtering through.

Sand underfoot, yielding soft to a level firmness, gave him the first sure knowledge that he was down. He stood on his four legs, easing his belly down to the sand, and rested.

Here in the hollows scarfs of vapours unfolded slowly all about him, slowly ascending, condensing, gathering in closer, until dune was lost to dune in a near world of mist.

He made his way limping blindly between them, treading the sand down in a clinging-particled dampness, unsure-footed among the hidden dunes: waded through mist-shallows that eddied past his flanks, silvering their amber scales with a chill and shivering wetness.

Mortal hunger drove him on: there was nothing to eat. Twice he plunged his head down and there was nothing but his own foot-tracks sucking and sinking under the mist. The third time he found the feather again, or one like it, blue-green on a little bank and furled: on its tip a pearl of clear water which, even as he watched it, fell and pierced the sand.

With the rock cliff somewhere behind him he went steadily on, nosing his way from dune to dune, and as he judged in the direction from which the bird had come. But in the twilight mist all places were alike, each dune he passed by a replica of the last until he was afraid, almost, that he might come to the rock face again: he might have circled the earth round and returned to the place, straining to see.

But it was his ears, before his eyes, that reassured him: a sound of water, the far trickling. And yet so faintly heard, he checked his running stride to be sure.

Closer, now.

He discovered it eventually on rising ground: a shallow rivulet, shallow but deepening; narrow but channelling the sandsoil as it ran, undermining its little banks so that here and there they fell, and were sluiced away under the mist in a moment.

He followed the way of its bank upstream, lengthening his stride on firmer ground that became a brushing of grass-tufts underfoot, soft-stemmed, and the darker-hued earth between springy to tread, moving into taller, closer grasses, rising tall into reeds growing in and out of the water itself until a thicket of leaves brushed his face and checked him.

On the far side of the thicket he heard the sudden crashing of some heavy creature's withdrawal and felt himself observed, aware of the mist thinning, the outline of the trees showing through grey and green. He felt the return of the sun's warmth on his spine and at the same moment, somewhere to his left among the nearer trees, a bird began a repetition of three notes, and was answered from across the stream.

His foot went down on the edge of a hollow among tree roots, warm and dry as if some creature as big as himself or a little bigger had lain here and moved off unseen at his coming. Eyes watched him: yellow eyes and brown and green regarded him and turned away, eyes in the trees and the thickets, eyes in the grass itself, and close to the running river surface.

Dappled brown and white, a new and slender creature splayed forelegs delicately wide to drink: lifted its head alert, prick-eared: regarded him, and resumed its drinking.

He made his way on down through shade into sunlight

again, pushing through a fragrance of white-flowering grasses that met above him in a pale green cool to the water's edge. The bird called again, and was answered across the stream. He straddled his legs firmly, squatting, and lowered his head to drink. The water was so clear, he could see the colouring of his own head scales, purple and amber, and the leafy trees growing there downwards, shattered into a thousand pieces at the first touch.

The water was cool and sweet to his tongue: spring-water; he had not known how thirsty he was.

When the mirror of it cleared there was another creature there reflected from the opposite bank: first as a bronze quivering as the water quivered to a stillness: then slim and straight as the reed-plumes, sapling-skinned as the young trees.

From a contemplation of this he lifted his head unhurriedly to regard the thing itself.

Across the bright span of water, onyx eyes looked directly into brown.

—the adam.

2

The Man

ARE you Elohim?

It was the splendour of colouring more than anything that captured Adam's wonder, to fetch the water about his thighs at one plunging stride, breath indrawn with the surprise of it and staggering, but never shifting his gaze: the sun-amber and orange, and the purple-hued folding of the wings in pairs, three and three.

—Eloh . . . im?

The word came back over the water, as the echo of his own question.

—'hovah-Elohim . . . Adam gasped, and reached for the bank. The grass stood up between his fingers. Pressing palms down he thrust one knee up, dripping . . . the Lord God. And now he was close he did not think it was the Lord God. He stood upright to shake himself, and for all its shining brightness the head came no higher than his knee. And yet a voice called me . . .

—Else it was the bird, Adam said.

His mouth rounded fleetingly for the *h'wee-ee* whistle-call, formed *wé-e-na* in a sigh of breath as his hands spread the sky out: *h'wee-wéna*, the bird. But it was not the bird that had called him Adam.

The dragon at his knee withdrew lazily, backing from the water's edge, hooded eyes watchful of the pattern of foliage

where the bird had sounded before. *H'wee-wéna* ...
Adam's eyes followed its gaze, seeing nothing but the green
leaves; and yet compelled to look.

Silver in the midstream turned both their heads back: a
little quick splash, and the surface rings there widening out to
break against the reed stems. On the far bank a leopard
crouched low to lap, amber eyed, and had come with no
sound at all. The gazelle had gone a little way farther
down.

—You are not ... Adam said, and stopped. He looked
at the dragon again, but it gave no sign that it heard him.
... like the others, he said.

He looked at the magnificent thing, and looked back at
the beauty of the gazelle and the leopard, not far from her.
And he said again you are not like the others.

—So you say.

—You have the Word, Adam said: like the Lord God.

—And you also.

—I?

But the beast moved from his side before he could question
the thought, leaving him wonderstruck to stare after it, the
broad tail thrashing right and left into the grasses and gone:
no more than a restlessness of the low fronds to show
where.

Adam ran a few paces knee-deep in the grass, cupped hands
and drew breath to call: and stood. How shall I call you?
shining one, wandering one ... Sudden as the ripe fruit it
had come, the bright fruit shaken from the tree; gone as the
wind itself through the bending grass-blades—but whither?

He made the *h'wee-ee-ee* whistle-call instead: and the bird
answered him now a third time close at hand. A moment,
and his eyes found it yellow on a pink-flowering spray:
yellow and blue as the little wings spanned for flight, no more

than the spread of his fingers. The spray dipped once and
lifted, and was empty. More blue than yellow on the wing
to his outstretched hand, the bird ringed his finger lightly to
perch, little head cocked, a bright eye watchful: and through
its beak a wisp of pale stem. He had not seen the stem until
now.

—Has the Lord God given it you? Adam said.

For meat, he supposed: and he watched, still, to see how it
would eat such a thing.

—Eat, then. Go on.

But it hopped on his finger to face the stream, the stem
held as before. He lifted his hand and it flew off, swooping
low over the water, two birds, a bird above and a bird
beneath, wing tips meeting an instant briefly at the surface
then apart: the gazelle's head and the leopard's lifted up, and
the blue gone in high among the little leaves; the little topmost leaves that stood on the air, shot through with sunshine,
and the blue between was the sky blue: Adam could not tell
if the bird had alighted there.

Shading his eyes, he could not tell.

And then, at the water's edge again, he forgot his purpose
for another thing remembered. He dropped to his haunches
with a hand down and kicked his legs free over the bank to
sit and recall it: the remembered shock of his first crossing,
the step down on to the surface, and then his foot trodden
clean through the shining skin of it—the breathless clenching
of his bowels—the sharp cold slap of it—

He edged forward and set the sole of his foot on the water,
tempting it. He dipped his foot and wriggled his toes.
Then he suddenly laughed, and across the stream the gazelle's
head came up at the sound. The leopard had gone, somewhere over among the live oaks, under shade. He filled his
lungs to call the leopard up and then, suffering a change of

mind, called the gazelle softly instead. But she would not cross the stream, timid at the margin, and his throat was too dry to call again.

The sunshine pricked his skin, sapping his strength out moist and salt on a finger tip carried to his tongue. He looked about for shade, but idly, detained by the pleasure of water cool about his ankles.

The drooping of his eyelids opened his ears to a marvel of smaller sounds. The continuous lap-lapping of the stream itself, the *thán* ... And the drowsy random pipe of birds, curiously muted on the still air ...

A humming in the grasses everywhere, unseen and murmurous, which he could not name ...

And then the discovered rhythm of his own breathing ...

It was the drouth in his throat that drew him to his feet at last. He cast about him for fruit to slake his thirst, but on this side of the stream found none. He made three paces uncertainly down the bank where the edge shelved down, and paused. It was here that the beast, the wandering one, had come when first Adam had seen him. Lying on his face, he tried to drink as he had seen the one and the leopard drink. But it went up his nose and choked him.

The third time he found a way, stemming the flow with his hand, and drank until his breath gave out.

—*Thán-eve*, Adam said.

Living water, the stream of life: because it flowed in an urgent pulsing under his skin, he could feel it, the running sap, quickening him to stir again, to move and run on the soles of his feet lightly, trying his renewed strength on the numb air. But he lay a moment to name it—*thán-eve*—and then he sprang up.

He crossed the stream back carelessly, breaking the silence with the commotion of his going: he alone moving when all else was still for the heat, gone under shade, under leaf, underground. Nothing moved but the stream behind him, and his own shadow small and shy at his feet.

Adam, moving upstream at a trot, the river on his left hand, heard the leopard through a wall of rushes on his right: the crown of a sapling agitated violently above the reed-plumes. He broke through and came upon the leopard stripping the tender bark below with claw and fang, and tumbled it nose over tail in among the rushes laughing, Make way! Make way! before it had properly turned at his coming. It struck out once and he caught and pinned it, fingers gripped deep in the fur. And then, loosing his hold, he crumpled its two ears in his hands until it rolled over and purred: and tiring of this, left it and went on alone.

He left the rushes and the riversound behind him and plunged deeper into the garden, running freely, easily, through the dappled tree-shade's flickering light and shadow, the hair-ferns feathery past his knees, through into sunshine that splashed the grassglades with vivid flowering colours, past the hanging fruit clusters, purple and amber as the dragon's scales.

He ran until the stream water he had drunk slowed him with an aching heaviness. He relieved himself in a golden arc and reaching overhead as he stood, broke off a handful of the purple fruit and crushed it in his teeth.

The fruit clusters above his hand jostled in a wind that blew cool and pleasant on his face, and rustled the leaves whispering. He stopped eating and turned his ear to listen, still.

Afar off in the wind he seemed to hear his own name called: and this time it was neither bird nor dragon, and he threw the fruit down and ran with the wind towards the sound.

3

The Lord God

EVERY TREE of the garden in which there is fruit, the Lord God said, I have given you for meat and for food. But of the tree of the knowledge of good and evil, you shall not eat of it.

There was not one tree, but two. Adam, lifting his eyelids, warily, through his lashes saw brightness fall from the air: a green dell and two trees, the second a little beyond the first. But it was upon the first that the brightness fell. It was as if the breath of the voice itself moved among the leaves and ruffled them, so that all the time they caught and lost and caught the light again like the blinking of innumerable eyes: a glittering to draw his feet down, and fascinate. On the first tree the leaves grew closely, overlapping. To discover the fruit, Adam pulled a bough down bending, and held it: and the fruit underneath was yellow, and soft to touch, with a sweet smell. And this was the tree of the knowledge of *good* . . . and *evil*. And he said the names to himself, Good and Evil.

—The day that you eat of it, the Lord God said, you shall surely die.

Adam let go the bough and it sprang back.

—So be it! he said, if ever I taste this fruit. And he said, Lord, I fell in the water. And a little bird no bigger than this stood on my hand when I told him.

—I have given you dominion over them. The birds of

the air, and the fish, and the dumb cattle, and every living thing that moves on the earth is in your keeping, Adam. Look after them for me.

There was no bird, nor anything moving in the dell. Only the silence flowed back in a green cool. Save where the one shaft of light fell upon the tree, it was dim to the eyes: the blossom of the second tree showed as a pale whiteness, indistinctly seen. From the dell on every side the ground rose steeply in banks overhung with leafage, so that there was no way in or out save the way Adam had come walking with the presence of the Lord God: the one narrow path steeply down, secret between fernbanks. It was by this path that he turned back.

He went as the voice led him, among the many trees again, breathing the forest air as he climbed above the dell higher, towards the sound of the river running, high ahead. A bird of bright plumage sudden as a cry winged clear of the trees, and somewhere a creature called for which Adam had no name, *ariff—riff—riff* . . . and he would have liked to call it up to see it.

—Behold, the Lord God said.

Where the trees ended the land lay tinted with colour spilled over from the evening sky, and the river where it ran was no more silver but gleamed a heavy red-gold, and held its depths secret. Here was no grass, but the earth face brown under the sky. And when Adam stood and looked it was the same everywhere as far as the river, and as far as the distant trees ahead: everywhere save by the river itself. Only beside the river and along its margin grew reeds waist high: and yet seen closer, unlike the river-seeds Adam knew, not plumed, nodding with a heavy red-gold crest.

—Every tree in which there is fruit, the Lord God said, and every herb bearing seed, I have given you for meat.

The seed grew close in the crest, in tight clusters. Fingering them, Adam plucked a handful, and bit it in his teeth: and it was good.

—And every herb bearing the seed of its own kind, whose seed is in itself, I have given you to replenish the earth. But first you must till the ground, and subdue it.

Underfoot, the earth was warm still from the sun, dry and brittle to walk on; and yet when Adam knelt, curious to try his fingers through it, the soil clung and came up in a darker moistness, damp. And he remembered the mists, how they had gone up from the garden everywhere and moistened the air chill like the than feeling; and hung everything and his own hair with shining, and afterwards had returned to the earth in a rain. And he had looked for it again and not found it, and this was where it had gone. Till the ground, the Lord God said: and subdue it.

—Elohim tell me: how shall I subdue it?

—Till the ground first, the Lord God said, and work it. Then you must sow the seed, and keep it safe, so that the herb of it will be meat for you again.

And he said, I will teach you, Adam.

In the dying light only the street of the thán was certain, the than-eve where it lay gleaming: the river beautiful, and the darker mass of the trees over beyond it. Under the nearer trees also the shadows gathered, sealing up the garden in a mystery, holding its depths secret as the river did, and strange.

Somewhere behind Adam as he stood a creature called plaintively, which he could not name, *riff—riff—riff* . . . and was quiet.

He shifted a little and stood on one leg, aware of the night air on his body, and it was as if it had been himself calling, out of some mood that was neither cold nor hunger, nor thirsting, and had no name. Lord . . . Even before he whispered it, without knowing why he whispered, turning in the darkness to the presence of the Lord God, the thought came to him that he was alone.

—Elohim . . . ?

—My son.

In the darkness Adam sighed, smiling, and rubbed the flesh of his arm. The stars came one by one to the surface of the river, and the pale moon floating. He moved his feet, glancing back towards the shelter of the forest; turned back a little way, and hesitated. Will you come with me?

—I am with you always.

He went on then in under the black branches, thrusting the boughs of them aside to pass through, stumbling among familiar things: ferncrunch underfoot and the dry bracken smell of it, smooth tree bole against his palms, and the rough kiss of the fronds. He smiled again at the startled hustlings his passage wakened close at hand, the companionship of small creatures scurrying and pattering out of his path. As his eyes grew accustomed to the want of light he went more surely, learning to distinguish shadow from shadow, and the deeper pools of the hollows before his foot trod into them. The furriness of catkins, brushing his arm, made him think of the leopard, and he stopped on the thought and drew a long breath to call it up, shattering the night. There was no answering call, and when he would have called again his jaw locked in a yawn. There was moonlight enough by now to show him he leaned on a bank tall with grass, in a grove. He yawned again, pressing his eyes, and surveyed it. There was a place under the bank itself where it was level, and he trod the grass down in a circle, kneeling to smooth it with his hands.

Before he was properly asleep the leopard came to him, coming through the night with no sound at all, he heard nothing. Lying on his back, he looked up and saw the amber eyes on the bank. A cloud passed across the moon, above the treetops, and he heard the leopard drop down. He felt the weight of it in the grass beside him. His outstretched hand told him of the comfortable purring through the warmth of fur, the claws that stretched out and withdrew softly, gently grazing his arm.

Half in his sleep it occurred to him, for no reason that he could name, to wonder where the dragon had gone.

4

The Sabbath

IT WAS the hand of the Lord God that wakened him.

The night and the leopard were gone. Through green-leafed branches white clouds unfurled on the same sky that was blue again, familiar as the chattering birdsong. The same sun thrust its many fingers in between the leafsprays, here and there in the grove where Adam lay, blessing the white flower and the red and lifting their heads; touching his own arm where it lay outflung with warmth, the hand of Elohim on his arm to stir him.

He stretched himself out to his full strength, hands clenched above his head, listening to the birds; laughed to hear them, and sat up, and scratched himself, and smelled the morning air. The grove looked different by daylight. The bank at his back cast a long shadow and at the edge of it, half in, half out of shade, the grasses were newly linked with gossamer, sparkling, as it were a star fallen dew-spangled. And beyond this another, but torn and broken, the grass pressed flat: which, while Adam shifted to consider it, straightened and came upright. He watched first one blade and then another lift itself and stand upright again, floating the filmy thread loose.

He walked over and himself trod the grass down under sole of foot, and stood aside to watch: and it was so: in time the blades righted themselves, the same. So he knew that

26

this was the way the leopard, the spotted one, had passed only moments before.

He could have called the leopard back; it would still hear him, he knew.

Instead, he followed the signs where they led him, the rising grass-blades and trodden earth, following where the leopard had gone out of the grove through the morning forest, until he came out of the trees and lost the signs altogether among the multitude going down to the fields of the river valley; where in a broad street the earth held the pattern of pad and hoof, mingled and overlaid.

Most, he could tell, were of the cattle *b'hemah*, the heavy-footed, deep with their bulk and slow; and the long-necked *zarifah* among them. The split-foot deer had come this way, also. And then afterwards, lower down as he went, he found the mark of the shining one, which was neither bird nor cattle, as he remembered it from the river bank before: the wandering one.

The track was uneven in depth and puzzled him until he went back and made his own alongside it, leaning on one foot, light on the other. And it was like this, limping, that he had seen the dragon come down to the water's edge to drink.

In sight of the river Adam looked for the amber and purple, but there was only a brown bear there, and several deer: a little roe with no branches at all, and eyes like the brown *roos* pools in the forest. Adam passed between bear and doe with a hand on each and threw himself down willingly to drink. He washed himself clean of the grass smell, freshening his eyes from sleep, and shook his hair back to see. Across the *thán* in the far shallows cattle lay about like grey stones with only their hump backs above the surface, and eyes watching sideways. He crossed over among them wading and looked

27

back, and there was a second doe like the first—*Roosah*, Adam said—walking delicately beside the river. He was hungry, and began to look up into the trees as he passed beneath them into shade again, taking the fruit where he found it.

Half the day until the noon heat he went as the spirit led him, roaming the wooded crests and valleys through fen and field, thicket and parklands, to the uttermost parts of the garden. He found fruit such as he had not tasted, soft-skinned as the doe's neck to his fingers, yellowing to the leaf, birds as beautiful as flowers and flowers beautiful as birds, whose fragrance filled the air with the presence of God. He looked down on a pride of lions in a valley, and named the *re'em*, the unicorn, when it passed him in the way, and heard the ass braying to the echo in the hills.

At noon he stood at the limit of the garden and looked out on the silent wilderness of Eden. *Havilah*, the place of sand round about, rising brown and flecked with green, strewn with stones like grey cattle as far as the sky wherever he turned his eyes.

White in the sand at his feet he found a stone half hidden. He took hold of its smoothness, considering it, and raised it up, and it came loose so suddenly that he staggered. He stood it upright in wonder and it was like a tree trunk of stone, as thick as his thigh. One end of it was broken off to a splintered roughness. The pangs of hunger came again and he let it fall, and it was hollow and dried out.

He listened, and there was nothing. No breath of wind: the trees behind him were still.

—Elohim!

The sound went out from him, to and fro in the wilderness, Elohim, lohim, ohim, ohmm . . .

Under the sky, something moved.

A flash of orange among the dun rocks, which caught and lost the sun.

Sun-amber and orange rippling, poured down between the rocks in a brief torrent of colour, and vanished.

A moment, and he saw it again nearer: the flashing scales of the long tail swerving, travelling down close to the sand, swaying to the one limpfoot, and the purple-hued folding of the wings in pairs, three and three.

Adam went a little way into the sun to meet it.

—Where have you been?

The dragon's head lifted as it came, onyx eyes slanting up to his face, narrowing against the sun.

—To and fro in the earth. It passed without stopping, so that Adam had to run to keep up. And walking up and down in it.

In the first shade of the garden, under the fringe of trees, the beast rested: so still it might have been without life. Why did you call Elohim?

—I was hungry, Adam said.

Slowly, in an awakening of surprise, the eyes opened again.

—Have you no meat?

Adam nodded, yes. All manner of fruit—there are trees all over the garden. I ate some fruit which the Lord God gave me on my way here. And he said, But I am still hungry. Why do you limp when you walk?

—God knows your needs, Adam. He will not suffer you to want for anything.

Leaf-shadows slid across the scales from purple into amber as the head moved again, twisting back towards the edge of sunlight. Do you know what that is?

—A stone, Adam said.

—Not a stone . . . Put your hand on your own thigh: take hold, and feel the flesh of it. And beneath the flesh the bone, like the bone there in the sand . . .   So are all creatures made.

Adam could feel it now, in his own leg, it was true.   He went to look at the white bone in the sand again, conscious that the dragon watched him.   He stood it up and it was taller than himself, such as of no animal he had seen in the garden yet.   He was going to ask what sort of beast this could be; but the pangs came again, more sharply, and he said instead, Will the dry bone satisfy me?   Or shall I suck it in my teeth?

And yet when he considered the thing again, it was in truth as if some creature had eaten and gnawed it.   The dragon's tail flicked once, lazily, and was still.

—Do you not know, that the flesh of the bone is meat indeed?

—Is it? Adam said.   But he could not imagine it.   He left the bone there and returned to the shade, glancing up into the nearby trees, but there was no fruit in these.   He said, I don't know . . .   The Lord God said I could eat freely of the fruit trees; he said nothing about flesh and bones.

—Did he not say, I have given you dominion over the birds of the air?   And the bird was in your hand . . .

Adam smiled suddenly to remember it.   He made a movement with his hand as if the bird stood even now on his finger and he loosed it again, yellow and blue over the waters of the than.   He saw that the dragon waited for some answer, and shook his head.

—The flesh of the fruit, I know.   If there is some new thing for eating the Lord God will tell me.   He will say, I have given it to you for meat.

And he remembered, when he said it, that the Lord God had said of the new reeds by the river, the herb bearing seed, *I have given you for meat.*   He had forgotten it until now.

He glanced back over his shoulder and the dragon was still there, a flowering of colours in the dappled grass, and then lost to view: *Levi*, wandering one; the wanderer in the earth, *levi-i-g'wána*. And it seemed to him as he went that Jehovah-Elohim had heard him when he, Adam, had called: and had sent the levi-i-g'wána out of the wilderness to put him in remembrance of the seed-ear of the river. He was glad, then. He followed his own tracks back, returning above the valley where the lions had been and were no more, and his feet through the grass startled a bird to a chance, tuneless note that broke into full song behind him: as it were his own soul singing to the pace he walked to, long after the sound of the bird had diminished and was lost to his ear.

He went without haste, staying his hunger on whatever fruit came to hand in passing, so that it was the cool of the day before he came to the river again. He crossed the shallows and followed the bank upstream to the place of the nodding reeds and walked in among them, plucking the ears and husking them between his palms to eat: watching the river how it ran, and held its depths secret.

In the river the stars came one by one, he counted them until they were beyond numbering, and lay on his back to consider them again in the far and beautiful patterns of the night sky above him, above the nodding and golden reed-crests whispering secrets about him, the little winds rustling, and things moving from silence into silence.

There was moonlight enough, when he walked through the forest again, to find him the grove, and the grass-hollow under the bank there. He cupped hands to his mouth, tired as he was, and called the leopard.

He made the grass flat in the hollow as before, and gathered fresh from above the bank, breaking off the stems to spread it down, and called the leopard a second time.

He curled himself down and listened to the forest, and opened his eyes again to the moon, waiting and listening. But the leopard did not come.

Half in his sleep he stretched out his arm and there was nothing but the loose grass there under his fingers. Memory stirred in him with the far sound of the river, moving his lips to whisper it, Elohim, Elohim ... And in the stirring of the night breezes in the forest all about him was the answering whisper, my son, my son.

5

─◆─◆─◆─◆─◆─◆─◆─◆─◆─◆─◆─◆─◆─◆─◆─◆─◆─

The Adamah

THE THIRD DAY, in the long shadows of the morning Adam walked alone beside the river again, through grasses spiked with cold, climbing until the first of the river-reed corn stood against the sun. The line of the forest on his right hand fell back, giving place to the brown and brittle earthfields, open to the sky, which the Lord God had given him for his own: to work it—*you must till the ground*—and keep it safe.

Pacing the edge of the forest away from the river he came upon the place where he had walked with the voice of Elohim and found his own tracks there overtrodden where the cattle b'hemah had come and gone, and the ground spoiled.

For a long moment, he considered this.

Then he went on at a slow trot between forest and earthfield, patterning the brownsoil underfoot behind him, his own land, Adam's land, Adam-wána, the *adamah*, saying the word and trying it, loosing his breath and breathing deep, and footpierced stumbling, broke his stride with a cry.

He held his foot in amazement, questioning the sensation sharper than water. It was as if his life beat all in the one foot. The blood ran down scarlet between his toes so that he forgot the hurt for the lovely colour of it, twisting his foot to see and he nearly fell. There was a shell-flint shaped like

one of the great shoulder scales of i-g'wána, more edged than
the leopard's claw to finger. Adam carried it a little way in
his hand, limping like the dragon, and dropped it again,
limping on the side of his foot until the brown earth took him
among shrubs and under small shade, and the landfall ran
down before him into living green again, a steep valley.
The forest spilled over its side and followed the line of the
valley down. He could look over the close mass of the treetops and see no end to it.

He walked the second edge of the field along the valley's
rim towards the sun, up to the farther trees, and came upon
tracks again: and now, looking back with the sun behind
him, he could see where they had beaten a street across the
adamah from forest to forest. Cattle tracks: but there were
others besides, not of b'hemah, yet like them: and yet so
much the greater that Adam dropped on knee and palm to
marvel. He set his hand in one of the tracks: one, and the
full spread of his fingers could not span it! Not b'hemah—
but *Behemoth*! as it were All Cattle, such a one as trees that
walked . . . The earth under Adam's palm was trodden
down to a hardness like stone. It would yield no living
herb.

He knew then what he would do.

He continued on more slowly for the heat, and for thinking, heedless until the river checked his feet. He lay to cool
his wrists and drink, and washed his foot clean of the blood
that had dried hard and dark, and the soil clinging to it.
Here the than ran swift and deep, he did not think any
creature could cross it here. A fish slipped through his
fingers and was gone. He saw another swerve away.
When he was refreshed he broke his fast among the river
corn, wandering down through it, blowing the husks from

his palm. When he came out of the corn again it was at the lowest corner of the field, which was his starting point, and he had trodden the adamah on every side and marked its uttermost limits, the length and breadth of it: forest to forest, and valley to than.

To keep the ground safe, he must enclose it.

He began in the same hour at the edge of the lower forest, where the shade was like a cool leaf frond laid against his skin, bowing the lesser branches with his weight until they snapped with their leaves and tore away from the tree bole. He stacked them between the first two trees that bordered the adamah into a thicket. To these he added stalk and stick and stem, thrust through between, such as he could break and gather with his hands. By the heat of the day, when he rested, he had sealed as many trees as the five fingers of his hand.

When he rested, he became aware of the eyes that watched him, everything he did.

He lay back, his head against a bough which he had broken down and left, unable to free it altogether, and the eyes were high above him peering down through the leaf-light, small and bright. He lay quiet, and it ventured a little lower: a small tree-creature neither bird nor of the earth, bush-tailed dark and white, tail up dropped and ran along a branch nearer. Adam lay quiet and it sat on the broken branch at his shoulder, considering him. He had to laugh then, and it moved away nimbly, eyeing him: and came back.

—How shall I call you? Adam said.

It put out a small forehand on to his wrist, a step not completed, hesitant, so little and light it was as the brushing of a brown leaf.

—Little one, Adam said: bush-tail . . .

Over his wrist, on to the branch again, and sat.

—Come, I will talk with you, Adam said. Do you know what Elohim has shown me? I'll tell you . . . shall I? I'll tell you everything in my heart, if you like: all the things I mean to do here, you shall know of. Then you'll be wise: wise as i-g'wana!

And he said, Wouldn't you like to be as wise as i-g'wana, little bush-tail?

He stretched up lazily, coaxing the creature with his finger tips and a soft clicking of his tongue. But it remained at a little distance.

—Listen, then! And I will tell you three things too wonderful for me—no, four, which I have seen this day . . .

It was the movement of Adam's foot that attracted the creature down: the stirring of his heel on the dry leaves. It came down the broken bough in little rushes, poised on the edge of flight, head up alert, nose twitching, sniffing the air. The scent of the man, which at first had alarmed, grew familiar. The voice cadences no longer troubled it: the rise and fall continuing to lull awareness until they became as much of the forest as the everrunning river. By the man's heel, among the leaves it uncovered a shell fruit, which it had itself buried there before.

Adam, telling of the dew-cold grasses up to the adamah— marvelling anew at the tracks of Behemoth—the scarlet blood out of his own foot—the way of the fish in the river, which lived and breathed beneath the surface—almost, Adam was persuaded that the bush-tail heeded, and understood his words, watching him over the fruit it nibbled, nodding as if to say, Tell me again of these wonders!

—The cattle would return and spoil the seed, if I sowed it in the open, Adam said. So Elohim has given me the first branches of the trees to build me a hedge; to shut off the forest above and the forest here below, and to keep the adamah safe from the valley.   And the river will be like a hedge, as well . . .

Adam drew his knees up and clasped them, looking to survey the first of the hedge where he had made it, sure that neither cattle nor beast of the field would break through.

—Do you think the Lord God will say, It is good . . . ?

Almost, Adam was persuaded that the little creature understood his words, nodding with the shell fruit fast in its forepaws sitting, to consider the matter, how it should answer him.

The bush-tail nibbled and spat out a fragment of shell, nibbling and nodding to gnaw out the flesh of the fruit within.

6

The Axe

ADAM was thirty-one days in making the lower hedge.

He numbered the days with stones and flints, gathered from the adamah and set aside: and because Elohim had blessed the seventh day, and sanctified it, he numbered them by sevens. Each evening he set down a stone to mark where he stood, so that the interval between was the work done that day, a length of hedge completed. When there were six stones, he laid a seventh beside the sixth at daybreak and rested from the work all that day, wandering through the garden as he pleased, wherever the spirit led him, in the presence of the Lord God.

At first, when the small branches came easily to hand, the work scarcely tired him, or put him to thought. He sang and whistled to the birds and stood to watch the coneys in the valley, and the long-eared hares which sat so still he could look and look and not see them until they moved. He paused to laugh at the tree-creatures, flinging a shell fruit for joy of their nimble descent; and in the noon resting gathered them about him to learn their ways, and named them each after his kind. Or else he left the hedge and walked by himself through the corn, among the stalks to consider them, how they grew: so that he might learn of Elohim how to scatter and sow them when the hedge was made. Or slow-footed with the heat, drew life afresh from the living river-water, lying face down on the bank. And it was there, where the river ran deep with fishes, that he first saw the length of scales slide far below him as a shadow in the filtered light: the four-legged river-creature scaled like Levi-i-g'wána, which he called *Levi-a-thán*, leviathan. Or he would chip with a flint at a shell fruit to open it whole, or sometimes at a scrap of tree wood for no purpose, watching the shadows lengthen, watching the leaves for the first trembling of wind, listening for a voice to call his name: until there was no birdsong nor riverrunning, no creaking of the upper branches nor far cattle lowing that did not cry, Adam! Adam! to his ear.

After the first evening, the leopard no longer answered his call.

—Can he build a hedge with hands? I-g'wana said. Has the spotted one the Word, does he walk and talk with God, that he should think himself equal with Adam?

And he said again, Has not God given you dominion over them?

So Adam went and tracked the leopard down under the live oaks, over beyond the river to the very end of the swampland, so far it could not have heard his call at any time; when he called it now, closer, it came out of the long grass obediently to him. He fetched it back with him under the grass-bank that evening, but it troubled him all night with restlessness, and long before morning he let it go.

At first the work was scarcely tiring, but then by increasing his efforts he made it so, disregarding the playful bushtail and no more singing, husbanding his strength to struggle with a branch too thick for his strength to snap, too heavy to carry: and snapped it, and carried it away on his shoulders with a fierce triumph which a moment after dwindled as the river-water through his hands, leaving him empty, and his purpose forgotten.

And then they would return to him again, the moods that

were not hunger, to be quieted with eating the fruit, or corn, or the white herb root; not thirst, to be quenched in the thán; nor the heaviness of eating and drinking nor anything that he might ease of himself, save by a wilder and more furious labour.

He watched the whirlpools below the riverfall, how in the midst of the turbulence only they had a stillness: and so it was with him.

And then he would return to the adamah and work again, driving himself harder and more fiercely through all the daylight hours, falling asleep the moment he lay under the grass-bank without waiting to know whether the leopard came or not; sleeping the night dreamless, and waking impatient for the new day. Yet for all his labouring, the interval between stone and stone was each day less. The lower branches and underwood stems, where before they had been plentiful, were each day fewer for his stripping, so that he was obliged to reach and climb higher, and carry his search wider and deeper into the forest to fetch the wood back, until the day came when he had collected no more than a small heap at noon: and he said, What shall I do now?

He lay under shade, then, and loosed the strings of his legs, knowing a slow pleasure in their aching, relaxed: and remembering, reached to twist the sole of his foot in his hands where the flint had pierced it; and knew that it was healed as the other.

Over towards the open valley a chital cried, and he knew that it was the leopard, moving to find a place out of the sun, that had disturbed it.

He split open a shell fruit to eat and a blue and yellow bird flew up between the trees, it might have been the same that stood on his hand, a wisp of stem in its beak, not for meat but for the making of a nest high up.

And he said again what shall I do.

The thought came to him that Igwana, who was wise in everything, would know this also: and with the thought he moved to spring up. But the movement slowed in doubt. The dragon came and went as he pleased, and answered no call. Nor were his tracks as the tracks of the beasts and cattle to be searched out; the levels of the garden and the high ways of the trees and the underwaters of the than were alike to him. He was winged, also. And Adam wondered, suddenly, whether Igwana could fly.

He said it aloud, I wonder if he can fly?

He wished the dragon would come, so that he could ask him. But it was useless to call. And Adam might walk the garden through to the far corners of it and never discover him, he knew.

Thinking of Igwana, wishing he would come, Adam set a shell fruit on a stick of wood to split it open and the mood came again, if not Igwana then the leopard, and he drove the flint in his hand down with force and smashed the shell with its fruit beyond eating and split the stick underneath. The leopard was in the valley, quite close, because the chital called. He could have fetched the leopard and made it stay with him, but he did not want to make it stay. And he remembered the bird in his hand, how it had flown off when he let it go.

He tried to free the flint, and could not.

And so it was with every creature, which came to him freely, and stayed a little, and afterwards returned to its kind.

The flint had pierced through the stick and wedged fast in the ground, he could not free the stick either.

He sprang up and straddled it, curving his back to take hold with both hands, and braced himself, and clenched his teeth. A moment he stayed, curved with power as a young sapling forced down. And then, with no warning, the stick with the flint came free, unleashing all his strength to fling him violently backwards to the ground, his breath expelled with a loud cry that started a flurry of wings over his head: scamperings of tree-creatures upwards.

The shock of it, as much as the alarm he had caused, released Adam's laughter so that he could no more hold it than his breath. For a little while he lay helpless. He held the stick still gripped in his right hand and presently lifted it, and knew the weight of the flint still wedged through the end. And then, as he considered it narrowly, the knowledge came to him, what it was that he held.

He set a scrap of wood upright and split it from end to end.

He pulled a branch with its spray of leaves from the heap and sheared off the spray.

He swung the flint axe in his hand like the slicing claw of the leopard, like the tusk of the hairy boar, and an excitement possessed him to set his feet running back through the forest within the hedge to the branch, the branch which he had broken down and could not free: hacking the whitewood chips flying until it fell at his feet.

He swung at a woodstem to hew it out, to see if he could, and the flint came away from the haft and fell at a distance. He found it and made it fast in the haft stick as before, chipping the woodstem until it split through, and dragged it after him with the branch to fling them on the heap. He cut down others where he found them, stalk and branch and the sapling trees themselves, such as had resisted the strength of his hands, working with the axe until it broke altogether: and then with a sharper flint, with a stouter stick made another, better than the first. The cool renewed his strength. No tiredness, but a want of light to see by, stopped him that day.

The third day after the Sabbath, which was the thirty-
first, the lower hedge was finished. Igwana came down the
side of the adamah to see, the iridescence of his scales bright
against the dun earth.

—It is good, Adam said: isn't it?

The dragon's head slid round unhurriedly, considering
the length of the hedge along to the river; onyx eyes lifted
to mark the height of it, a great way above.

—Why ask me? There is One to distinguish between
good and evil: even God.

—Evil, Adam said. He turned the axe in his hands,
fingering the suppleness of lianas which he had bound about
it to keep the head secure. I know all things are good,
which Elohim has made. But what is evil? And he remembered the tree of the knowledge of good and evil, and
the fruit, of which the Lord God had said, You shall not
eat of it.

—Is the hedge evil?

—Why do you tempt me? If I say it is good, and it
seems to God evil, I am a liar. The dragon lowered his
eyes to rest on Adam's face. You tell me first: what does
Elohim say?

—I ... cannot tell, Adam said. The sun full on the
amber scales troubled his eyes, and he turned his face aside
and moved back a pace into shade again, and dropped down
to sit. He had wanted Igwana to come, hoping he would
come and see the finished hedge; and now, almost, wished
he had not. I cannot tell.

—No? But you have walked with his voice in the
garden from the beginning; and has he not given you all
knowledge? Surely you have sought him in the cool of
the day, to ask him about the hedge also?

—Though I sought him, Adam said: and he drove the

flint head of the axe into the ground between his two feet.
. . . yet I didn't find him.   There was no sound but the far
river.   And he thought it was true that he had not found
Elohim.   But it was not true that he had sought him.   There
was no sound but the river; and then a dry rustling as Igwana
moved down under shade beside him.   The dragon's eyes
watched him, he knew.

—His ways are not your ways, Adam.   His thoughts
are not like your thoughts; or mine.   You cannot search
them out, or understand them.   Do you think that God,
who made the sun and the moon and the stars and the earth,
has nothing to do but to care for Adam only?   And if it
please him to forsake you for a season, will you complain?

—Adam.
—I hear you, Adam said.   Behold I am foolish.   I am
like the dumb brutes, without understanding.

With the movement of the sun the shade grew less, so that
the light fell on his face again; but he did not move.   He
closed his eyes but there was no darkness, the warmth and
colour there still under his eyelids: the warm breath of Igwana
at his shoulder.   Foolish, Adam.

—For what purpose have you made the hedge, if not to
safeguard the adamah?   And you can see with your own eyes
it is well done: neither beast nor cattle shall be able to break
through.   What more do you want?   Foolish Adam.
Has not God created you after his own likeness?   How then
can you say, I am like the dumb beasts.   Rather are you like
God.   For remember, you were made in his image.

—Adam.
—I hear you, Adam said.
—In all the earth, tell me, where is your like?   In whose

44

hand but yours alone is the wonder of the axe? which makes even the trees bow down before you. And you made it.

—Yet not I, Adam said: but Elohim.

He opened his eyes again, and the axe shaft was there between his feet, the flint head buried fast in the ground. But the dragon Igwana was gone from beside him.

7

Behemoth

HE SAW the downward rush of the leaves first, so high up that he looked for bush-tail, for some tree-creature alighting from a flying leap: but the bough did not lift again, it was held down, quivering.

In a grey coil as thick as his own arm to the wrist.

A moment, and it tore off the young green leaves in a sheaf, loosed the bough to swing up and bore the sheaf down: and Adam's eyes with it.

The spread of ears like great wings! Like great grey leaf fronds flapping!

The massive whitebone curve of tusks!

The tremendous height and mass of grey! Such as a greystone hill that moved in the foliage.

Such a one as trees that walked.

Dumb for wonder Adam stood, watching how the grey coil curled under between the tusks and fed the leaves into the open mouth below. As the sapling to the forest cedar, so was the tusk of the boar to the tusk of Behemoth.

Sudden on the air, the forlorn cry of a jackal startled them both, man and beast: loosed Adam's tongue to exclaim; drew the great head of Behemoth round in a slow, unhurried movement. The trunk, uncoiling to reach up for leaves again, was lowered empty. From its height above him, the beast regarded the man, and was still.

—With what shall I compare you? Adam said.

He ran forward and measured his own height against one leg like a cedar tree, like an oak, and set the palm of his hand to try the roughness of grey skin, wrinkled as tree bark.

—Or among all the beasts of the field, which is like you?

He laughed for delight and the strangeness of it, and walked all round the four legs where they stood, passing between them under the belly of it, and so to the head again.

—Behemoth, oh, wonderful! There's none like you in the garden; none. Hasn't God made the moon among the stars?—so much greater than all the others!

He beckoned the trunk down and took hold with his hands, leaning himself on it: and it swayed him as a reed in the wind, and yet with gentleness. One eye—unless he stood back or walked round he could see only one—blinked and regarded him. An eye round and small in the great grey head. An eye wrinkled and wise. He let the trunk go and it curled slowly away, to rub the smooth bark of a half-grown tree. And then, in a single upward movement, plucked it with its roots out of the ground.

Adam's mouth formed *Elohim!* with no sound. The tree was as thick as his own thigh above the knee.

—Now I am ashamed.

He ran forward to the tree where the beast had thrown it down at a little distance, and took hold; and he could scarcely raise it from the ground.

—If I say in my heart, I have made me an axe, I am strong ... the Lord God has made Behemoth to shame me ...

—*This mighty one, this Behemoth: has he the Word?*

It was dark now. It was Igwana, Adam knew, but could not see him. Behemoth was gone with no more than a light splintering of twigs, a rustle of leaves, as a great grey shadow among the forest trees, marvellously quiet. Has Behemoth the word? No. Who then has the Word, which is more than strength, and breadth, and height? God.

And Adam.

And Igwana, the dragon—was it Igwana who spoke? Adam turned his head, and listened.

He could hear the river again, when he listened. And a rustle, such a little rustle underfoot that was Igwana's departing. Or else it was the wind among the dry leaves.

—Or did I speak of myself? Adam said.

He listened, but there was no answer: nor any voice in all the forest save his own.

8

The Storm

I WILL NOT fail you, nor forsake you, the Lord God said.

It was as a dream that Adam remembered it: as a dream or a vision of the night, whose images vanished in the moment of waking, slipping from memory as the fish through his fingers and gone. And then afterwards, in the way of dreams, returning to haunt the fringes of his mind. So that now, lying snug under the shelter of leaves that he had made and listening to the drip, drip of the trees outside; smelling the morning fresh and new, the rain-washed earth and the living green; hearing the river close behind and narrowing his eyes to where the one tree lay charred black and splintered, lay out from the forest across the brown adamah; Adam puzzled his mind to remember.

All day it had been hot: the sun like an open eye staring, forcing his eyelids down. Long before noon the birdsong had died away down into the cooler depths of the forest out of hearing. Above, in the upper branches, even the chatter of the tree-creatures had ceased in a quiet.

He had climbed to the top of the adamah to work on the second hedge, at the edge of the upper forest, and afterwards with the axe had made himself a shelter of branches over towards the river bank, and roofed it with leaves. For a little he had rested there out of the sun and then, rising again to cool himself at the river, had fetched reeds and grasses and spread them in the sun to dry.

Through the long afternoon the face of the sky pressed down on the earth, as if to drive out the air between. Throughout the garden leaf and frond were still. He had laid the grasses and the reeds within the shelter for a sleeping place, where he would sleep sound; where he might lie in peace and watch the stars come out in the high firmament, over the open valley and above the forest and the wooded hills; where he would sleep soft with the conversation of the river for company close at hand. But when the shelter was finished it was still day, and he went back to work at the hedge once more.

It was the heat that stopped him.

Heat, and the drouth of mouth and nostrils, the stinging salt moistness in his eyes, and the running of every part of him in a sweat. He had gone walking a little way to look for the cool winds of evening, and found no breath. Only the stillness, and a silence that beat at his ears, bringing the pangs again, wakening the moods of discontent. A restlessness troubled him, drawing his feet aimlessly here and there, like a voice calling, indistinctly heard: drawing his feet in a sudden and urgent running, he could not tell where, stumbling, breaking his stride to listen to the silence again. As a calling that teased his ear, a voice imagined, seeming to summon him now into the forest; now to the open adamah again; and then to the dark mouth of the valley. When he stood still there was no sound.

He broke the silence himself with a shout: and it was as if all the garden was still to hear him.

He made the bird's *h'wee-ee-ee* and the leopard's deep-throated call, and the *riff—riff* of the jackal dog: and one after another the calls went hither and thither down the unseen valley, farther and fainter, beating away in echoes and lost.

Only the silence came back to him.

In all the garden, no voice save his own.

He called once more, *Elohim!* And the silence came back.

And if it please him to forsake you for a season . . .

—Elohim!

. . . will you complain?

—Elohim, Adam said. And he whispered it, uncertainly, Elohim . . .

No voice save his own; none.

Only the silence.

And then it came, like the beating of wings over the valley: a great wind rushing through the treetops, bending the bush shrubs all one way. The force of it came on Adam so violently that only an instant bracing of his legs saved him from being thrown down. Bowing his head before it he could at first hear nothing but the roaring in his ears and the rushing trees. But then, lifting his head so that his hair flew back, he knew what it was, and covered his face.

It was bright as high noon, the heavens themselves split apart with one blinding light that sealed his eyes: as though a great multitude stood all about him, the very earth trembling at the voice of the Lord God walking upon the hilltops.

Whether the wind enfolding gathered him up to walk, or whether he walked in the spirit only, he could not afterwards tell.

It seemed as if he were lifted up in the presence of God, so that his soul looked down and saw Adam prostrate on the earth. And then as though he walked the wind at the right hand of Elohim to survey all the hedges his handiwork in a moment of time, and the creatures one by one as he had named them, each after his kind; and himself telling of the wonders of Behemoth; the miracle of the axe which Elohim had put into his hand.

And he remembered, now, how the voice had spoken out of the wind, saying, Do you marvel at these?

—You have been faithful, Adam: I am well pleased with you. If you will trust me, and keep my commandments, you shall ask what you will, and it shall be done for you.

—Jehovah, I promise—I will keep your commandments for ever! Whatever you tell me, I will do. Only let me hear your voice . . .

—Be still; and you shall hear it.

—Elohim, Adam said: oh, Elohim! it's been like hunger and thirst with me, looking for you in the garden, listening for you in every evening wind, hoping you would come. And my soul was cast down, because I couldn't find you.

—Trust me: for I am with you always. When you have spoken my name, have I not heard you? I will not fail you, nor forsake you: wheresoever you go, the Lord your God is with you.

And he said, Do you marvel, Adam, because I showed you the uses of the axe? Behold, a greater wonder than this I will show you.

It was as if the heavens split apart with a blinding light that joined earth and sky, as by a silver cord brighter than the sun: as if the sky fell down on earth with a shout and the stars came tumbling all about him, brighter than noon day, and the forest shook itself, and the bush shrubs cringed. As if the veil of heaven was rent and the countenance of the Lord God Jehovah shone down in glory and spoke with his voice, and clapped his hands together from the corners of the sky.

At the edge of the upper forest in the same moment the

one tree charred black and split open, falling down stricken across the adamah. Out of the blackness of the night, in the place where it lay, there came bright flames, two and three, like little tongues lapping: and then the hissing of the rain.

Adam, trimming a long branch of deadwood with the axe and whistling, whittling the end to a sharpened point, sitting astride the stricken tree, set the point in a split to hold it still, and remembered. He set the axe down and collected the wood chips by handfuls as the Lord God had shown him, in a heap about the split where the pointed stake was set. It was thus that the burning light had struck down from heaven: thus it pierced the tree: thus, and a finger of smoke like the river-mist rose as he spun the stake in his hands, faster and faster. A spark like a bright star leaped; and another; and the heap sprang into flame, hissing. For a moment it burned like a little sun, and died.

Adam smelled the smoke, and thrust his hand presently into the warmth of the ashes, and snatched it away; laughed and marvelled, and laughed again.

The second time the smoke rose again but he could make no spark. He cut the stake presently sharper and heaped the wood chips higher, and the flame leaped up, so that he fell back from the heat of it and the sparks pricked his skin.

That night, and each that followed, he made himself a fire before his shelter in the open and lay warm beside it, watching the marvel of the little quivering flames, like little tongues eating up the deadwood; and the movement of the shadows on the ground.

9

Adam by Himself

THREE NIGHTS, and four, the jackal dog s'gala curled nose to tail by the fire side, one eye watchful if Adam should stir; one ear attentive to the man's voice; pricked at the mention of his own name, *S'gala*. Three days he trotted at the man's side as his shadow, and four lay loose-tongued under shade to watch the hedge grow longer, branch by branch hewn and stacked through the long days until evening.

The fifth day, in the morning, his tracks were gone away up between river and forest.

Adam followed them; but not far. When he found the second track the same, running alongside the first, he turned back to the adamah.

Here on the high ground each strike of the axe sounded twice over, near and then far off in the valley. It was the echo, he knew; and yet almost he could imagine there was another like himself, who worked with an axe there somewhere out of sight. But if he paused to listen, there was no more sound. If he ran down to the valley to see, to be sure, there would be none there: he knew it. And yet at each stroke he made, though he swung the axe again with the rhythm he worked to, still his ear waited for that other strike to answer.

In the mornings he might have refreshed himself at the river close by his shelter; but he chose more often to walk

54

down beside it, down past the willows and the falls to the lower shallows to lie cool in them with the cattle and the deer round about him, watching them, and sometimes putting out a hand to touch them, and calling them by their names. He would linger there sometimes until the water grew chill to his skin, and sometimes climbing up to the adamah again, gathered fruit as he went but not from hunger, or delayed along the lower hedge to discover if any creature had broken through since last he looked; finding no sign; knowing he would find none.

One evening, sleepless from the shelter, he walked at the edge of the forest, walking slowly for no purpose but to breathe the night air. When he looked down over the dark mass of the trees in the moonlight, he heard the leopard call from the valley. Before he reached the landfall, finding a way among the shrubs for his feet, the leopard called again a second time, and he laughed softly.

—I hear you!

He threw back his head and drew breath: and then, while his chest was still extended, the call was answered from the lower forest.

It was not the echo. For a moment it seemed to Adam, easing his breath out hushed in surprise, that the leopard had taken wing as a bird out of the valley to the place—swifter than a bird.

But there were two: and he stood silent and alone, listening to their call and answer, and call again, drawing closer together. But he saw neither. The last call was from far down the valley. In the long silence that followed it, Adam walked back, and watched the track of the wind as it passed over the treetops, the dark mass in the moonlight seething, as though it were somehow part of himself, sighing, restless, never still, never at peace.

And then, feeling the wind, he remembered that the Lord God had said I am with you always; and he said it aloud, Always, and lifted his face to the night sky. He felt the wind's breath on his cheek again, and remembered it, You shall ask what you will, and it shall be done for you.

—Lord God, I promise . . .

—Ask what you will.

But he stood, looking up at the unspeakable beauty of the firmament which the Lord God had made: and not the stars only, but the sun for a light by day, and the moon by night. And he thought that Elohim had given him meat, and drink, and every tree pleasant to the sight and good for food, and all creatures both great and small to be in the garden with him: he could think of nothing in all the earth which Elohim had withheld from him. Even the axe and the fire, Elohim had given him, which he had given to no other living creature: even the Word, so that he could both speak and understand it.

—What more shall Adam ask, Lord?

He put his fingers to his cheek where the wind blew softly, and then, dropping his hand again, walked on along the edge of the valley where the land fell away into darkness, among the peace of shadows. It was from there that the leopards had called. But he forgot the leopards and went on, considering the open valley side, wondering how he could fence the adamah there.

—Nevertheless, the Lord God said: it is not good that the man should be alone.

Adam, walking slowly back towards the shelter once more, stretched out his arms wide and . . . yawned . . .

❖❖❖❖❖❖❖❖❖❖❖❖❖❖❖❖❖❖❖❖❖❖❖

10

The Woman—I

IGWANA the dragon lay in a covert of ferns that concealed every part of him except his eyes. He lay with the scales of his underbelly pressed to the earth, so still he might have been without life; with his wings folded back, watching.

Above him, above the fern tendrils curling close, the forest cedars soared up straight and tall into a far height of green leafage, laced across a blue sky. Below him was the tree of life, the flowering of its blossom shining white in the radiance that filled the dell; and a little way apart from it, over against the mouth of the dell, the tree of the knowledge of good and evil, every yellow fruit turned to gold with reflected light. But it was towards the tree of life that he looked.

Beneath it, was the visible presence of God.

With hooded eyes, warily, Igwana watched: so still that a green and jewelled spider clambered over his talons one by one undisturbed. Only once, he made a small movement: once, when the face of God turned as by chance towards him, the dragon lowered his head withdrawn in the same instant; yet so smoothly that not a frond of the covert was displaced. Under his eyelids, he felt the brightness pass over him, and dim again. He lay there hidden, the ferns greeny-brown before his eyes' cautious reopening, hooded over their smouldering change of colour. Only a slight, muscular twitching rippled down the bruised and purple scales of his spine. A small tear in the earth marked the contraction of his talons, under the lame and injured foot.

Presently, very gradually, he began to lift his head again.

The back of God was towards him now: all the glory of that familiar countenance towards the tree of life, which shone as if every leaf and petal were on fire. Now, at the tree foot, the pale shape on which the Lord God looked lay perfectly formed. And for the first time, Igwana saw what it was.

Very still it lay, and pale, the smooth skin luminous, like a new sapling in full moonlight, a creature fashioned like the adam to walk upright, and yet without life: the countenance tranquil as a stone. Beneath the sealed eyelids, the cheekbones were faintly shadowed where the lashes rested.

Igwana, watching, saw the presence of God pass closer, the radiant light drawn in from all the dell to fall full on that pallid face; saw the pale lips parted and the delicate shell of the nostrils quiver; and the breath of God like a flame drawn in, burning as fire beneath the skin, suffusing the cheeks with glowing colour as embers fanned by the wind. He saw the lips, the warm and ruddy lips, parted a second time, and heard their audible sigh. The eyelids fluttered, and were lifted with their lashes slowly, as a sleeper awakened.

The eyes were not narrowed, as Igwana's were narrowed; not hooded, nor contracted as his own contracted from that sun-brightness, but opened wide. Yet he looked only towards the back of God: but this one face to face. He would have opened his own eyes wide for the fury of it: and could not.

—I command you, Arise . . .

Quiet as he lay, the dragon's tail stirred behind him under the ferns, just the tip, the end-scales twitching: then stilled in disbelief. *It does not see him.*

It was true; at the sound of the voice the creature's face was lifted and turned, not towards God's presence there, but in a slow and wondering survey of the dell in which it lay.

—Arise now: and come . . .

At the lip of the dell the fern tendrils gradually closed back, spreading again in the empty space where the dragon had been.

In the leaf-thatched shelter at the top of the adamah, Adam stirred and opened his eyes. For a time he lay unseeing, only gradually returning from a depth to shallows of sleep, and awareness.

It was the hunger, he supposed, that had wakened him; and wondering why he should wake so hungry, he turned his face to the adamah and saw immediately that there was no sign of the morning dew—the dew had gone.

Long ago!

Because of the clouds, he had not known: the low white moving clouds swallowed up the sunshine and held the adamah shadowed in half-light like the first of morning. But the sun was overhead. He shook his head in amazement, but it was noon, and he drove his hair back through his fingers.

—Such a sleep!

His first thought was for the hedge. He reached out hastily for the axe beside him where he lay, and a spasm crossed his face. He caught his lower lip in his teeth. With his fingers, gently, he explored the tenderness of flesh in his side, looking to see. The hurt beneath his finger tips.

And then, lifting his head again and turning his ear to be sure, he heard the voice of the Lord God in the garden.

He had to take hold with both hands to stand upright.

His right side was as the sole of his foot had been, the day the flint pierced it: throbbing as if his life beat all in the one place. This time there was no blood; no break in the flesh at all. He stood against the corner post of the shelter. When he lifted his eyes, he saw that the clouds had come down in a white mist over the adamah between himself and the lower forest.

From out of the mist, where he had heard the voice of the Lord God, there came one walking upright towards him.

A moment, Adam stood transfixed. And then, losing his hold on the post, for weakness slid to his knees. The brown earth swam in a haze, in dizziness; the life-blood pulsing in his side, in the darkness of his eyelids; light as the footsteps that drew nearer, slowing, and ceased.

The feet were as his own; and yet how unlike. Neither roughened nor stained, nor marred in anything, but beautiful; without blemish. And he laid his head to the earth between them.

—Neither bow down, nor worship, the Lord God said: for it is your own flesh.

—It is an angel, Adam said.

—It is your own flesh, which I have taken from your side while you slept, to make a help meet for you. Take hold of her hand, Adam; and arise ...

As in a dream, Adam obeyed.

—See now, I have created you male and female, to be one flesh: so that you shall be fruitful, and multiply, and replenish the earth. And with my blessing I will bless you, man and wife I will bless you; I will give you rain in due season, and the land shall yield her increase, and the trees of the garden their fruit: and you shall eat of them to the full. And I will give you peace in the land, and you shall lie down, and none shall make you afraid.

Her living hand, in Adam's own, clasped palm to palm, warm and strange . . .

And yet familiar . . .

—Flesh, Adam said, of my flesh.

And he cried out suddenly for the marvel and joy of it, Bone of my bone, and flesh of my flesh—at last! And he held her one hand in the two of his own and said, How shall I call her? From my *Ish*—from my own being—she is made. She shall be called *Ishah*, because she was taken out of Ish.

Ishah, the woman.

Her eyes were as the sky, blue and bright; the cloud-mists lifting and the sunshine swarming in the garden all about them, the birdsong renewed, and the tree-creatures chattering at the edge of the forest.

—Ishah, she said: and laughed.

The Woman—II

HER EYES were as the sky, blue and bright; quick as a sparrow with their darting, curious glances, athirst for wonder. She lay beside him over the river bank, pointing down.

—Adam, she said. Ishah.

And immediately, her head was turned to follow the ripples of the midstream down.

Watching her, Adam forgot his hunger, and the soreness of his side. For she was more beautiful than the gazelle to look upon. When she moved, the sunshine touched a sheen on her skin, glancing over heel and thigh, and the hollow of her back: but it stayed in her hair. His own hair, remembered in the water below, was dark as the night. As the night and the day, so were their two heads together.

—Ishah I see, she said: and Adam I see ... And she turned her bright head. ... but where now is he? who brought me here.

—Jehovah-Elohim, Adam said: it was the voice of the Lord God. His presence went up with the cloud, I expect. And thinking of it, he remembered the storm, when the voice of the Lord God had spoken out of the sky. And he said, Into heaven.

When he spoke of heaven, she lay back on one elbow and lifted her face. So far above!

—Not so far that he cannot see us. His face is towards us, always.

The brightness compelled her lashes down, and she lifted one slender arm for a covering. The movement drew the little buds of her two breasts upward, her wrist against her eyes.

She said, Is that his face?

—It is the sun, Adam told her, smiling. It is not God: but he made it.

—He told me to rise up, she said. And when I came up to meet you, he was with me. I heard his voice, but I saw no one beside me. Why couldn't I see him?

—Your eyes are not able to look upon the sun. How then can you look upon the glory of him, who made it?

But she was looking at Adam, and set her hand between her thighs in wonder. She put out a hand and touched him; touched his bearded cheek and laughed; then her own; and glanced down to compare their faces in the water again. When she leaned down, the daybright tresses slid in a cascade over the slenderness of her shoulder, against her mouth; and she tossed her head to fling them back.

She drank as he showed her, hollowing her hands in imitation of his. In her eagerness she choked a little and drew breath in surprise, widening her eyes until Adam laughed aloud. He was sorry he laughed, it made his side hurt again, the throbbing. Her laughter followed his own immediately, and she plunged her hands again to drink, tossing her hair back.

She was quick to learn, swift in understanding; never still, threshing the water with her feet into glittering spray, scattering wet footprints behind her down the bank to cry out in question at something seen on the far side, that slid down into the water at her approach, nosing down to the depths—

Leviathan, Adam answered; though he saw no more than the ripples where it had gone: Leviathan, it must be. He followed more slowly, content to watch her zigzag progress, hither and thither as the bee among the sweet herbs; to measure his foot beside her smaller print, yet the deeper because she ran; to look back and see their two tracks together, how they intermingled. Among the first oaks he turned aside out of the sun to rest his side, calling out to her, but she was too far to hear. Then she saw, and came running back.

—What is it?

—I am faint from the sun, Adam said. Or it may be from lack of meat, I've eaten nothing this day yet. It will pass in a moment.

—What is meat? Show me, and I will fetch it for you.

He raised himself to point out the fruit trees to her. She ran down and presently returned with two great clusters. He took one from her hand and broke off the fruit, eating them one by one until the first ache of hunger was stilled; resting where he lay, on his left side. Her eyes were on his face. The cluster he had left in her hand, she still held, uncertainly. He laughed again and bit a fruit through, swallowing half: and half he put into her mouth with his fingers.

—Taste and see!

Afterwards, he went down with her among the trees there and showed her other fruit good to eat: the green and the red, yellow and white, the heavy breadfruit and the locust tree; that which must be broken out of the shell, and which peeled to the fingers, and the sweet brown clusters which grew high up, and could be gathered only with climbing. He showed her where the tender shoots were to be found, and the herb roots; the bees' honeycomb and the scarlet berries of the forest. He brought her to the green dell in the midst of the garden to point out the tree of the knowledge of good and evil, of which Elohim had forbidden them to eat; and he told her.

—Lest we die.

She ran forward and he caught her wrist.

—I want to look at it, she said.

—Don't touch it.

—I will not touch it, she said: only look at it. She went a few paces and then, seeing that the man remained, came slowly back. But I know this place . . . She looked to one side and the other, from the moss mound at the tree foot to the dark leafage overhanging the banks, topped with ferns, and suddenly cried out, Adam!

—Adam! It was *here*—from this very place, that the hand of the Lord God raised me up!

But he knew it already. She asked him, How can it be? How could you know, before I told you? And he said, Because of the tracks.

He showed her those she had now freshly made, which entered the dell a few steps and returned; and these others, the same, yet previous: he marked for her with his finger, how the new overlaid the old, which came the one way only, out of the dell. She knelt, and leaned down lower, hand on his shoulder to look more closely, and saw where his finger rested, a little pressing down of the leaf-mould, the white core of a broken twig, a dry leaf crumbled: whether by sole of foot she could scarcely tell; much less which way the step went.

Presently, she stood up. In the forest the daylight was already fading, the bright sunbeams softening to a mellow twilight. It was as if the garden had slept and began to awaken with stirrings, and voices. Listen!

And she said again, whispering it, Listen . . .

—Adam.

He lifted his head. He had gone a little way apart and squatted down as before.

—It is the dove, he said.

She wanted to ask him, What manner of creature is the dove? But he was looking at the ground again and suddenly stood, and walked down into the dell. In surprise she watched him go, walking slowly, with many pauses. She lost him among the deeper shadows, dark under the height of bank there; uncertain if she should follow; then saw him again as he stood upright, moving against the pallor of the tree blossom.

He returned as slowly, and she said, What are you looking for? Have you seen my foot tracks there as well?

—Yours, Adam said: and others beside them, which walked over yours.

—Of Elohim?

—Woman, how could it be! No, not of Elohim; one you haven't seen. Adam put his arm about her shoulders, turning her away from the dell. You shall see him presently in the garden—and every creature the Lord God has made, besides! Oh, Ishah—wait until you see them!

—Tell me now, she said, whose track it was. Then I shall know when I see him.

Adam's hand was on her arm. Levi-i-g'wána, he said. But I call him Igwana. See how dark it is! Come, we will go up to the adamah again; if we hurry we shall see the sunset.

Because of the hedge in their way, he led her by the hand across the forest, guiding her feet by unseen paths familiar to him, the many voices of the forest always ahead and behind them, hushed at their passing, then shrill again: the owl, and the langur, and the shrill cicadas; and each time she pulled on his hand to ask, Is it the dove? Is it Igwana?

They were too late for the sunset; the adamah, when they came to it, rose dark as the forest, with only a faint lightening of the sky to show the line of the trees at the far end. In the open they climbed more quickly, side by side, until Adam brought her to the shelter. He left her there and went up a little way past the unfinished hedge, where he knew there was deadwood lying. He gathered an armful by touch and made his way back.

—Ishah . . .

—I am here.

She lay within the shelter. The fire, when he had kindled it, flickered on her face, her chin on the curve of her arm. He thought she slept; but when presently he stooped in under the thatched roof, treading softly not to waken her, she shifted to make a place for him.

The flickering firelight played over her hair, and he put out a hand to marvel, how lustrous and soft it was; how unlike his own. Beyond the fire, high over the adamah he saw the first star, and he wondered if he should disturb her to see. Her eyes were closed.

He thought she slept; but her lips moved to speak his name.

—I hear you, he said.

—Adam . . . Why did the igwana go down to the tree? seeing that it is forbidden.

But they slept, both of them, before she could wait for an answer or he find any to give her; thigh by thigh and shoulder to shoulder, and his hand in her hair.

12

The Cub

FROM ABOVE AND AFAR, the valley fields in the sun were smooth as still waters, as the green and pleasant backwaters of the thán, the far grass beautiful as moss to walk upon. But close, the same grass grew taller than the horns of b'hemah.

The cub came uncertainly through in short clumsy leaps, with many falls, struggling with entangled feet. At first, his progress was slow for the frequent changes of direction, decoyed aside by every new scent and sound. He pushed his blunt nose against the stems to plunge again, prying the honeybrown fluff of his small head through to discover what lay behind: but deep in the undergrass all places were alike. His forefoot trod on a broken shoot. Its sharpness, pricking the tender pad, sent him tumbling backwards in alarm.

And then, struggling up again, sniffing the air, he found himself in an open tunnel, heavy with the boar smell; where he could move and walk freely, and the sun came through in standing beams.

Following the line of light, he broke into a gambolling run.

—It is s'gala, Adam said. Surely.

But he was not sure.

From the branch on which he sat astride, a little more than

his own height above the ground, he had no clear view. Yet s'gala the jackal, the same that had walked in his shadow, it was not. And he said, Else it's the hind.

The woman, lying farther out along the branch, had parted the leaves to peer down into the valley.

—It isn't the hind, she said: I have seen the hind.

In the morning shallows she had seen them, in the watering places of the thán, when Adam had named them at her question: creatures more slender, loftier, more delicate than this. And she said, It isn't the hind, and slid down from the branch to drop lightly.

Like the hind herself she ran down the valley side, far down before Adam guessed her purpose. But she ran where she had seen the creature last, to a thinning of the long grass; so that it was Adam, seeing the tunnel there and coming directly to its mouth, who came upon the cub first.

Though it came out of the boar run, neither was it *chaẓir*, the boar.

—Ishah! Come and see!

And he said, It is some new thing which the Lord God has made.

He sat with the cub between his two feet to consider it with delight, the harmless frenzy of its little teeth gnawing at his ankle until he cried out with laughing and pain, and set his hand between to prevent it. He heard Ishah's indrawn breath at his shoulder.

Though she came softly the cub backed at her approach: then quivering, sprang at her foot in the grass. She knelt and caught it up in her arms.

—Ah, just look! How still he lies . . .

—He's tired from so much running, Adam said: now he will sleep.

The woman bent her head, her cheek against the fur.

Her eyes were soft. But he is panting . . . What do you say? It may be he is thirsty.

And she said, Is he thirsty, Adam?

He was considering the creature, and how to answer her: whether it was from thirst or exhaustion that it panted. And then, seeing the woman's altered gaze go past him, he looked back over his shoulder.

—Ch'hora . . .

The head and shoulders of the lioness filled the mouth of the boar run, tawny flanks blending into its shadow, the head lifted a moment, watchful: yellowing with sunlight as the beast walked forward, so that Adam drew his feet back to let it go past. Ai, Ch'hora! Where are you off to by yourself?—they live together, Ishah, and keep to the valleys, until now.

But it went no farther than where the woman knelt; and stopped. The cub in Ishah's arms stirred to a waking protest and struggled.

—See how like they are! Ishah said. She laughed to compare them together, the great and the small. Isn't this one ch'hora as well?

—You are wise as the bush-tail, Ishah. Has Elohim made the lion like a jackal, or a fox?—to run in between your feet! Or will you pick ch'hora up in your arms, also. Try, then!

—Yet they are like, Ishah said.

—Loose the little one, Ishah: and see what he will do.

She loosed it, but before the cub moved at all the lioness had pinned it again, mouthing the loose skin behind its head; straddled it, and shifted her grip; and then, lifting it clear of the ground, carried it swinging limply between her forelegs with long padding strides towards the long grass. Ishah ran beside them until they went in under the shadow, entering the

tunnel mouth where she could not follow; and she turned back.
She put a hand behind her neck, under the hair, wincing in
astonishment, how it must be—to be carried so! Yet the
cub had made no sound.

Adam, rising to start up the slope again, looked back to
wait for her. The little one, she said: is it well with the
little one? And he told her, It is well.

—He has gone among his own.

Ishah would have tried the tunnel just the same, but he
called her to try another way. By climbing the slope and
following the ridge of the hills along, they would be more
likely to see the lioness again.

Ishah ran to climb breathless beside him, looking back all
the time. Didn't I say the little one was ch'hora too?
And you denied it. She made a scornful face, like Adam's
face when he denied it, *Has Elohim made the lion like a jackal?*

—Who am I? Adam said. I spoke of myself, but now
Elohim has answered us both: though the new one is little—
not so big as a jackal, even!—he is of the lions just the same.
And if ch'hora is strong and mighty among the beasts of the
field, yet he's no stronger, nor more mighty, than the hand
of the Lord God has made him.

And he said, thinking of it, Have you noticed, Ishah,
how among the trees of the forest there stand both great and
small? and yet the same as to flower and leaf? It's the same
with every green herb . . . have you noticed them? and the
way they are enlarged with growing . . .

And he stopped on the thought. Ishah—

But she ran up past him, calling back, Is the bush-tail not
wise?

He smiled. Not very wise.

—Then it is foolish. Is it?

—I did not say it was foolish.

But she did not understand this, and waited for him. Am I like the bush-tail, Adam?

And she said, Why am I.

—You have heard the bush-tail chattering in the treetops.

—I've heard them; but I couldn't understand them. What does it mean?

—It doesn't mean anything.

And then, seeing that she had stopped to consider this, he drew her on by the hand and said, But the forest would be quiet without them.

They saw not one cub in the valley, but two. The light was beginning to pale, the first soft winds just nodding the long grass-plumes whispering together. Adam lay watching, with Ishah beside him, the two cubs below, and the two lions with them; the one that gave suck, and the one that stood apart, watchful. It was Ishah who named the lions, male and female.

—Ch'hora, she said: and ch'horiyah.

They could not tell, from so far above, which of the two cubs it was that the woman had held a little while before, warm against her breast.

—Show me an angel, Ishah said.

Adam, surprised into looking at her, sought a reason for the saying, and found none. How shall I show you such a thing? Angels are not like the creatures of the garden, that we can go and look for them: they are the messengers of God.

—But you have seen them . . .

—No.

She was surprised, that he had not seen them. The day the Lord God brought me to you, you said, It is an angel.

It was strange, that he had forgotten so soon. He looked at her again: at the seriousness of her small face, shifting to the edge of a smile under his gaze, half smiling, puzzled for his answer. And he remembered how it had been then, in the hour that she came up from before the face of the Lord God, walking in brightness out of the mist.

—Your face ... *shone*, Ishah. There was a sort of light about you, exceeding bright, like—

And he said, Like the angels, I think; like the Cherubim ... Ishah said, Has Elohim taught you this?

But it was not Elohim, it was the dragon, the shining one. And he told her.

—Igwana.

—Igwana, Igwana, she said. Who is Igwana? who knows the angels by name, and walks freely round about the tree of knowledge—in the very place which the Lord God has forbidden us! Is he of the beasts of the field?

—No; no, not of the beasts of the field.

—Of the cattle?

—Nor of the cattle.

—Bird of the air?

—No, Adam said: yet, winged ...

And she said, Winged, yet not a bird: what manner of creature is he, then?

But for all her questions, Adam could not tell her.

13

The Blessed

BECAUSE they were two the work seemed light, a pleasant thing to spend their strength on, so that the days passed swifter than the ripples of the than, and the evenings came soon and unlooked for. Six days out of seven they fetched the forest branches down together to extend the second hedge, building it new along above the adamah, daystone by daystone farther from the river, nearer to the valley. They worked in the fresh hours of morning and the first of evening, breaking off to lie the noon heat out under shade, drowsy as the birds in conversation; or sprung by an impulse one would race back to outrun the other to the river bank; until the day that Ishah, turning her head to shout, fell headlong and swam as a fish; and Adam after her. When she said, See how Elohim has made us! We can come and go as freely in the waters as on the dry land.

It was the same day also that the woman first braided her hair, weaving a green band of the rushes to bind it behind her neck because it troubled her for its wetness; which afterwards she plaited with flowers.

The sound of the axe brought the langurs down from the forest heights in troops, swaying down the pathways of the treetops to amaze them with dizzy antics; ungainly on the ground to walk half as the man, drawing Ishah's quick and rippling laughter: yet gone in a breath in wingless flight

through the treeways again.   Sometimes the bush-tail came
down to take fruit at Adam's hand, the shell fruit from his
fingers; and s'gala out of the woodlands, two and three running in and out among the trees to frisk in the sun.   The pea-
cock stepped by them as the Lord God had made it: and even
the dragon, Adam said, is not more beautifully coloured than
this.

Behemoth came down also.

They came in the dumb noon when the forest was hushed,
slow-moving as grey clouds that drifted closer among the
trees.   And Adam touched the woman's arm as she lay.

—Behold one mightier than we: Behemoth, Ishah . . .
All my strength is not sufficient so much as to move his foot
from the earth it stands on!

He signalled the nearest of them to come closer, so that
she might more perfectly see.   But before the beast had more
than turned towards them, Ishah was up already from Adam's
side and running to meet it.   He smiled at her amazement,
remembering his own that first time: head thrown back to
gaze up, up, and the eager strides faltering . . .   Ishah cried
out, just as he had, for wonder.   Adam, Adam . . . !

He came beside her as she clasped the one leg round as it
stood, the leg like an oak tree, and it was true: it could not
be moved for all her pressing against it.   She fell back flushed,
and shook her hair back helplessly.

—Laugh, then! she said.   Only tell me, what is the
secret of his great strength?—that he is able to resist us so
easily—have you teased me, Adam? saying that all creatures
are subject to us?   How can we possibly rule over this—
mountain! Seeing that he scarcely knows whether I am
pushing him or not.

And she said, Laugh, then.

—Oh, Ishah.   Do you think you can do it by yourself?

even move Behemoth with the strength of your hands! But the Lord God, he shall move him.

She fell back, not understanding until Adam stepped past her and struck the beast's knee backhanded with a shout— *Up!* and the massive leg yielded, and was slowly lifted from the ground.

—Not that we of ourselves have any power: but Elohim has made them obedient to us.

Though he taught her many things; yet he learned from her also. In the first light waking she touched him to say, It is the Lord: he is calling us.

And then, when he listened, and smilingly told her, It is only the birds singing, she nodded and stretched out her arms.

—Didn't he give tongues to the birds? And who but Elohim has sent them to waken us?

Or of the bright morning she said, Elohim smiles on us; and it was so.

The woman it was who taught the langurs to fetch down the topmost of the fruit, the brown clusters, and the hairy coconut which broke open to sweet water and yielded at once both meat and drink; of whose split shell she made a vessel to bring water from the than, and gave Adam to drink in the noon rest; she who first climbed upon the broad back of Behemoth, and sat between heaven and earth swaying down beside the adamah with waving and laughter.

Because he wanted to finish the hedge, Adam let her go; disregarding her calls with the thought, If Elohim comes again, and finds the thing he commanded not done, he will be displeased with us. So he let her go waving and laughing, letting the strike of the axe answer her. She would know by the sound that he stayed. But then after a while, when she summoned him more urgently, he let the axe fall and went down to her.

—I have seen an angel, she said.

He found her across the river, still clinging high up behind the ears of Behemoth, half kneeling there. The beast stood patiently feeding, tearing leaves from the young green fringe of saplings against its front. From where she clung, the woman could see over them. Her face was towards the garden beyond: and then turned with pleasure at the man's coming. And she said, I have seen an angel.

—Where?

Adam crossed the shallows running. The saplings marked the beginning of the swamp, he knew, the lush and yielding fenland. Behemoth, with his great heaviness, could go no farther.

—Ishah, come down. Show me where.

But she shook her head. While I was calling you, it vanished out of sight.

And she pointed, and said, That way: afar off.

And then she said, Are you angry?

—I do well to be angry. Hasn't Elohim, even the Lord God, set apart one day in seven?—a time to work, and a time to rest from working? And you call me all the way down from the adamah, away from the work, to see—nothing! Make haste now; let us go back while there is still light.

She had not seen Adam angry. She looked down in wonder at his upturned face. But she made no move.

—Will you come down? Adam said.

—I cannot.

And he saw that she could not. She had got up by climbing first upon the beast's uplifted knee, which she had made him lift as Adam had done before, striking the leg to tell him.

She could not come down the same way. Nor could she, from where she knelt, find any way of bringing Behemoth's head round from the tender saplings, to turn back.

Slowly, as he perceived it, Adam began to laugh. Behemoth, who made haste in nothing, might remain here eating the young leaves through the evening until nightfall—until morning, perhaps! and Ishah with him. Adam thrust himself still laughing through the foliage to take Behemoth by the trunk and draw him round; watchful of his own feet, where the beast trod.

—Now I understand, he said, why you called Adam.

—No, but I did see an angel!

—Afar off, Adam said.

He guided Behemoth back into the river, to the deeper part, and half way across caused him to kneel; so that Ishah was able to slide easily down into the water. On the bank she shook herself, and caught her hair back.

—It was as a spreading of wings, she said, exceedingly bright: which I saw one moment, and was gone the next. And I saw one like ch'horiyah running beside it; like the she-lion, but altogether spotted.

Whether it was indeed an angel she saw, or whether the leopard, crossing the swamp at speed, threw up a waterspray shimmering in the sun, Adam could not tell. Though they went back, and she led him to the place, they found no living creature but the frog and the waterfowl there; and in the waterlogged ground, no tracks at all.

14

This is My Beloved

THE THIRD HEDGE, between the adamah and the open valley, they made of brushwood set upright between hewn stakes, which Behemoth carried down from the forest as the woman taught him, walking sometimes at his head, but more often riding high up behind the broad grey fronds of his ears, with a stick in her hand to guide him; so that Adam from afar off saw first the sun on her hair, and then the coloured flowers that decked it.

Often now, when the ringing strike of the axe sounded back from the valley, he smiled to himself, remembering how he had wished it more than the echo only; which though he had not uttered it, nor understood what it was his soul yearned after, yet the Lord God had both heard and answered.

—How was it with you, Ishah asked him, in the days before I came?

As well might she have asked him, How was it with the garden, before God made Adam? For he could not tell. The days were as though they had never been, when she was not with him; nor any joy of Eden remembered, which was not shared with her. Was there ever a day without the sound of her laughter? or her step beside him? or his name on her lips? Had he ever truly woken with no smell of her hair in his nostrils, with no rise and fall of breathing in the shelter but his own? Or had he ever gathered of the fruit clusters, and not by two and two?

Was the garden silent, in the days before the river chuckled down through it, and the first bird sang?

—When there was none beside you, Ishah said: and when you were alone.

And he said slowly, No; not alone.

—Was Igwana with you?

But he had forgotten the dragon.

—It is true that Igwana was with me sometimes: but Elohim always.

Sometimes, when she was absent from him, Adam tried to remember. When she had gone up into the forest for brushwood, or to the thán to fetch water; or when he made the gates in the hedges and Ishah, seeing no way in which she might help him, wandered away on some purpose of her own: then he stood a moment in the silence, wordless, and heard again the grasses humming, and the far riverrunning, and felt himself small under the sky; little beside the giant cedars of God. But even his awareness of these things was changed with the thought of communicating them to the woman: how he would afterwards tell Ishah.

Very lovely the grassglades down beside the river, the fountain fall of the willow trees, the flowering grasses starred with white petals so small the eye could scarcely tell them. Soft in sunshine, crisp in the morning, delicious and cool to walk in; cool as her hand's first touch on his own. Very beautiful the green leaves, high up where the sunshine broke through, softest, palest green of all the garden. It was a pleasant thing, and full of delight, to lie still under their shade at noon, to listen to the birds somewhere, here and there, and name each by his song to her question, half asleep with contentment.

For she questioned him always: of the birds' talk and the split hoof track, the spider's web and the bark-ripped sapling; of the crimson sky Westward, and the pattern of stars; the tree that lay charred and the suckling kid and the pollen-stained bee—What is it, Adam? What does it mean? The bubbles rising to the river surface, the dark-mouthed hole under the bank—Adam, tell me!

—Tell me.

And she would turn eagerly to him, demanding, coaxing, her small face animated, lips parted breathlessly, her quick eyes searching his face as if she would anticipate his spoken word: or in the close-wrapped darkness of the shelter, startled by the haunting owl, her mouth at his ear, pleading, imperious.

—What is it, Adam?

Imperious, when a new tenderness stopped his throat and delayed his answer half forgotten for her nearness' sake, the smell and dear touch of her, his life-beat under her fingers; when he was silent for wonder of the Lord God who made the thing so fair, and yet of Adam one flesh: his name on her breath, the image in her eyes—his own.

—Tell me.

As much as he knew, he told her. Though he smiled at her insistence, her tireless questioning, as often as he could he answered her willingly.

Sometimes, he could not.

What of the stars? Where does the rain come from? And the wind, where does it go? But these things are of God, Ishah. Content for himself with the boundaries of his understanding, Adam was not troubled, as she was, to ponder on these things or seek reasons for them. Elohim knows, he said.

As much as Adam knew, he told her. But for the tenderness in his throat, he had no words to tell of it.

There was a kid of the goats wandering from the hill pastures, which ventured into the than and was carried over the falls. Ishah saw it go. She was gathering seeds among the corn for the sowing, heaping them into a frond cupped against her breast, but when she saw the kid she let them fall scattered and ran to the bank.

Her alarm call and the splash of her dive brought Adam in haste from the adamah, his hand stained with the soil. When he saw the place where she had gone he cried out to Elohim for her: for not even Leviathan could swim there in the quickstream, above the waterfall.

He raced down the bank through the flying spray, his heart like a stone within him, straining to hear her cry above the roar of the falls, searching for some sign of her in the seething waters there, but there was nothing.

It was a great way downstream below the falls that Adam found her.

She was safe, treading water with the kid held up beside her; only exhausted with the effort of holding it. He swam to her side and took it from her, and set it upon the bank. Ishah smiled when he turned again, but her face was pale, and her teeth chattered with cold. He fetched her to the bank and carried her in his arms out of the water to a place in the sun, and he laid her on the grass there. He rubbed her feet and her hands until the colour came again, and smoothed her wet hair. And then, when he would have stood up, she locked her fingers in his hair to prevent him. Her voice was husky.

—The kid: is it safe?

—It is safe, he told her. But he said it harshly, and she lifted her eyes in the shadow of his face.

—It was foolish of me, she said.

—It was more than foolish. Woman, haven't I fore-warned you, to be ware of the falls? Or have you no eyes? —to see how swift the river runs there!

—I thank you, for coming, she said.

—Thank God!—if he had not kept you, you would have gone under the depths for ever! And so you deserve.

She let go his hair, then, and turned her face aside. It was for the kid, she said. And you are angry for this?

He tried to speak, and could not: only for answer caught her up to him, breast crushed to breast with the strength of his arm: but not in anger.

—Ishah! Oh, Ishah!

For this is my beloved, who was lost and is found again.

She had never been alone. She had never called, with no voice to answer her. The moment of separation, such as he had tasted, had no meaning for her.

—You—laugh? Adam said.

—To see you angry . . .

But then, when he would have loosed her, she clung to him with laughter and fierce tenderness and would not let him go; until he broke her clasp and himself drew her down to make one with the sweet-smelling grasses, the white petals crushed in their fragrance, in the sun by the river margin: the colourful dragonfly gone over them unheeded and the kid forgotten to its grazing. Once, she cried out, and the curve of her arm about his neck tightened. The kingfisher, brave blue over the water, swerved at the sound and perched watchful: but it was not repeated. Adam put his hand under her breast to feel her heart beating, soft as the dove in his palm; and remembered the Lord God who gave her to him. And she slept.

He went softly and broke off a bough with the leaves upon it, which he set upright in the ground to throw its shade over her. For a moment, he stood. Then he went down to find the kid again, and carried it across the thán lower down, where it flowed broader and more shallow, and set the kid down on the farther bank.

He looked back once more to the place where she lay asleep; and then, setting his face towards the hill pastures, began the long climb up, driving the kid in front of him, thinking that he would be back before she awoke.

15

⟡⟡⟡⟡⟡⟡⟡⟡⟡⟡⟡⟡⟡⟡⟡⟡⟡⟡⟡⟡⟡⟡⟡⟡⟡

The Temptation

THE FIRST THING the woman saw on opening her eyes
was the green-leafed bough upright, standing between herself and the sun.

For a moment she lay, puzzled to account for the thing:
as it were a little tree sprung up and sprouted within the hour
of her sleeping. Then she put out her hand to try it: and it
came rootless away with the first tugging. So that she suddenly laughed, and turned to look for him who had planted
it there.

—He is gone with the kid, Igwana said.

The shock of the voice—not Adam's—so close to her,
stilled her heart an instant. The dragon lay half hidden in
the taller grass over against the river, amber-bright scales
against the water where the sun made a street of flame: it was
a moment before she could distinguish his shape. Her heart
beat again with sudden violence. Not Adam, but *Abir*—
the angel close by her: the same that she had seen in the
swamp. And she thought, It *was* an angel; I knew it was.

She became aware, then, of what it was he had said. She
turned to look for the kid, and it was not there.

—Has Adam sent you? she said. And she whispered it:
and immediately remembered what Adam had told her of the
angels, that they were the messengers of God.

—Or are you come from God? she said.

—Neither from man nor God. I come and go as I please —as you do, surely.

She considered the truth of this; reassured to hear him speak again, as one might speak to another; sitting back on her heels to braid her hair. She wished he would rise up out of the grass, so that she might more perfectly see him—and spread his great wings out, as he had spread them that day in the swamp, when she had sat high up on Behemoth and looked over the saplings. Thus close, he seemed smaller than she remembered; no bigger than herself.

—It is true, she said, we often walk for pleasure in the garden; on the Sabbath, and in the evening. But the Lord God, he has made paths for our feet from the beginning. We walk as his spirit leads us.

—So do the beasts of the field: in the paths God has made for them. The cattle plod each morning down to the river, and each evening return in the mire of their own tracks; the fish swims up and down in the narrow thán the same, between its two banks. Even Behemoth, though they roam far afield, go and return always through the same forests at the appointed time, having no understanding of another way. But as for me, I please myself.

Ishah, listening to his voice, forgot her hair and was still with thought. Do we not please ourselves? she wondered. She had set Adam's bough upright again to keep its shade, and plucked at the leaves, doubtfully. Or is there some other way which we, like the cattle, are ignorant of? A spray of leaves snapped off in her fingers, and the sun broke through, and she looked at Igwana's wings again.

—Is it some heavenly way? she said.

The dragon lifted his head to regard her, drawing himself up from the grass so that for the first time she saw him plainly, the full magnificence of his colouring, and the scaled sweep of his tail.   And she caught her breath.   For a moment the amber eyes held her own, and then, with a slow, deliberate movement, the dragon turned his head to survey the river, and the lush green grasses along its margin; the lilies there, and the slender rushes, the rising woodlands and farther forests, and the outline of the green hills beyond: drawing her eyes after his gaze.   But it was as if he had forgotten her there.

—This is my heaven now . . .

And then he turned again, moving closer to her.   But your eyes cannot see it.

—Yet I can see it! Ishah said.

—As the cattle, or as the dumb brutes see it: without under-standing.   As the . . . bush-tail.

—Bush-tail!

Because Adam had said it before, *You are wise as the bush-tail, Ishah*; and she looked quickly at the angel, but he could not have known; and she dropped her eyes.

When she dropped her eyes she saw his talons in the grass, drawing closer: which were like no beast she had seen; nor any cattle . . .   More like a bird, and yet . . .

Winged, yet not a bird.

—Igwana!

Now that she knew who he was, she looked at him again curiously.   She had not imagined Igwana to be like this. *Levi-i-g'wána*, Adam had said, but where in the earth had he wandered, that she had never before seen him?

—We go openly, she said, before the face of every creature. And where we lie down to sleep, our fire may be seen of all the garden.   But where your dwelling place is, I cannot tell.

—I have told you: your eyes cannot see it, neither have you known.   I dwell where you dwell.   And when you walk in the garden, I am not far from you, Ishah.

But she shook her head in disbelief—How was it possible?

How could such a one pass unperceived, whose scales were brighter than the parakeet, and shining as the river enflamed? And then she remembered the footprints in the dell, which had walked over her own: and she suddenly shivered.

She said, Why did you go down to the tree of knowledge? the day that I was made . . .

—I have told you: I go as I please. All places are alike to me.

—But the tree in the midst of the garden! she said: in the dell, in the forest—which the Lord God has forbidden us!

—Has he? The dragon turned with the speed of surprise to look, first towards the forest, then to the woman's face again. Is it so? Has God said you are not to eat of every tree of the garden?

—No! And she laughed. Because if Igwana had been as close by her as he had said, whether openly or in secret, he might have seen her taking the fruit freely where she found it, and Adam with her. And she said, No—we may eat the fruit of the trees of the garden: only of the one tree, which is in the midst of the garden, God has said, You shall not eat of it, nor shall you touch it, lest you die.

She stood up, stretching her legs as she spoke, wishing Adam would come; conscious of thirst, the sun hot on her shoulders when she stood. I am thirsty! She walked across to the river. The dragon moved down at her side.

—The tree you speak of: is it more than another? Or is the fruit of it bitter, that it would harm you?

Ishah, kneeling at the water's edge, cupping her hands to drink, stayed them half lifted. The water drained away through her fingers.

—It is true, she said: it is like the trees of the garden to look at. And whether more than another I cannot tell. But what is bitter?

Waiting for his answer, she forgot her thirst. But he crouched low to lap as if he had not heard, the shining length of scales tilted down in changing colours to the brink, amber and orange, orange and purple, the beauty of wings close-folded like great leaves overlapping. When he had drunk his fill he withdrew backwards a little way, and rested on his belly. In the water the pieces of her face came together again, and were still.

—Tell me what is bitter, she said.

—Is this also hidden from you? Now I begin to see how much God has withheld from you. For how can you savour that which is sweet? seeing you are without the knowledge of bitterness. And as for the fruit, whether it is bitter or sweet, how will you know unless you first taste it? For unless you taste the fruit, you have no knowledge.

Ishah, listening to his voice, saw her own face in the water floating pale and strange on the gentle undulations of the flow, wistful and wise; it was as if she saw it for the first time. He said, Unless you taste the fruit, you have no knowledge . . .

You have no knowledge . . .

And she saw her face as Adam saw it, *You are wise as the bush-tail, Ishah*, and she had said is the bush-tail not wise? and he had said, *Not very wise . . . I did not say it was foolish.*

But it is not very wise.

You see the garden as the cattle, or as the dumb brutes see it: without understanding.

I have told you: your eyes cannot see it.

You have no knowledge.

Unless you taste the fruit.

—God has forbidden it, she said. Shall I taste the fruit, which God has forbidden?

The dragon flexed his talons in the grass, lazily. What is that to me?

And she saw her own face in the water, as Adam saw it.

—I will ask Adam, she said.   When he returns, I will ask him.

—Ask him, then.   But you know already what he will say.

She knew what he would say.   He would say, These things are of God, Ishah; Elohim knows.   And he would say, Angels are not like the creatures of the garden, that we can go and look for them.   How shall I show you such a thing?

She saw her face in the water, her own face, and yet not her own: in imagination shining with light, bright as an angel, wise as Igwana, with all knowledge.   She put her hand down slowly to break the spell of it: and the water's chill clasp closed on her wrist.

—But if we die!

If . . .

—You will not die, Igwana said.

His voice was distant, and she lifted her head.   He had gone a way upstream to the river's edge again, where the bank shelved down to the water.

—He said we would die, Ishah said.

—So that you should not eat the fruit.   For God knows that in the day you eat it, your eyes will be opened, and you will be as the angels, knowing good and evil.

—Good, we know already! Ishah said.

—And evil?

He entered the water as Leviathan did, easing himself down with no splash, soundlessly, the downward stream was scarcely disturbed.   She saw the surface close again over him, the last end-scales of his tail gone down in a bright ripple: and the river empty from bank to bank, as if he had never been.

Only the words remained, lingering on the still air of the afternoon: *You will be as the angels* ...

She suddenly dipped her hands to drink, cupping them with a little splash that broke the spell of it; laughed for the sweet cool of water on her tongue; swung her legs over to sit, splashing her feet to froth the stream, winced at the cold spray and laughed again, throwing her head back, and the garland of flowers she had braided in her hair flew out into the grass.

She went and fetched it, and began to fasten her hair again, sitting with her ankles in the stream.

Between her two feet the face came again, mirrored: and she regarded it seriously, braiding her hair. The sun behind her head made a halo of brightness there, and in imagination she saw herself shining in beauty like Igwana, and Adam beside her shining; lowering her eyelids to consider the picture she made. As the angels ... Adam and Ishah. And she tried to remember the fruit of the tree; but she had not seen it. And she wondered what it was like.

When she had finished with her hair, she withdrew her feet and stood up, looking to see if Adam was coming; but she could not see him. She went a little way down the river bank, uncertainly; and then turned back. I will not touch it. She began to walk towards the forest.

Only look at it.

16

The Fall

ADAM, hot from the long climb, swung his aching legs loose over a ledge of rock, grateful for its coolness. At first, coming up from the river valley, he had slackened his pace so that he should not tire the kid; but once among the broken hills it had outdistanced him, sensing the presence of the flock long before Adam found the first dung, or saw any movement. So he let it go on alone, waiting only to see it safe: its bleating once answered, when the horned she-goat leapt down from rock to rock to meet it. And now, having rested, he turned back.

The downward path was easier. But he was too tired to hurry. The sun, which had been behind him all the way up, was now full in his eyes; so that he presently turned aside another way where there were pine trees growing, making his own path down through them; the more slowly for the pleasure of their shade, the silent leaf-mould soft underfoot. He could have lingered there willingly until the cool of the day: but the thought of Ishah in the valley drew him down. And he thought he would rest awhile with her there beside the river, before they went back to the adamah again: a little while. And then the remembrance of it, the little work done that day until now, quickened his stride. He saw the bright street of the thán again winding far below him as he came out of the trees.

Coming down over the grass to the river bank he thought, for a moment, that he had mistaken the place. Not until he had swum the stream, and found the sheltering bough thrown down and shrivelled, the grass crushed where she had lain, was he sure. He called her name.

She had not waited, then.

—Ishah!

But she was gone, and he moved restlessly, unable to account for her going. Waking she must have seen the tracks, must have known that Adam had gone with the kid. The way of man and beast at the water crossing were plain to see, if she had looked for the tracks. And he cast about for hers in the grass; but it was difficult to tell in the grass.

Only at the edge of the bank was the ground soft enough to tell clearly: as if her foot had slipped as she entered the water—and he thought, She had gone another way to meet me.

But it was the dragon, not the woman, whose tracks were in the mud there; not Ishah, but Igwana, the forked talons pressed deep, the dragon, the shining one... Then he found the place where Ishah had been, the footprints, lower down, but at the river's edge again.

She is gone with the dragon.

The place was very still. His own shadow was still, tall beside the water; the water lapping gently under the bank, still in the midstream.

A scarlet flower, loose on the grass, puzzled his mind.

It drew his eyes for its colour, a flower in the flowering grasses: one scarlet among the many white. And he remembered that she had braided her hair with scarlet that day. She had made a garland, pricking each stem with her nail and drawing another through it, linking them in a strand. And

then, considering the one flower there, Adam dropped down
on one knee, and his shadow sprang small to his foot. It
was to drink that she had lain there. She had come no farther
than the bank. She had not crossed over with Igwana, she
had drunk and turned back.

Because he knew she must have returned to the adamah,
Adam found her tracks again easily, leading up beside the
forest. He went at a slow trot with no more than a glance
down as he ran. And he thought, She is gone back to the
adamah because it is a working day. And we have made
our own Sabbath by the river. He was ashamed, then, because he had been thinking of nothing but the woman and
the cool of grass: and she had thought of the work.

With the sun on his shoulders he remembered his thirst,
half wishing he had delayed by the thán to refresh himself;
half thinking to turn aside again; but he ran on. How shall
I answer Elohim, if Ishah works alone? When he glanced
down again he had lost the tracks.

For a moment he hesitated. And then, with growing
surprise, went back to trace their new direction.

She had turned abruptly into the forest itself, running—
the footprints smaller and deeper, with a longer stride. And
then after a little way slowing. There was a confusion of
signs, as if she had halted, then gone a short way to her right
hand, now to her left; as if she were lost or undecided. But
he did not think she could be lost in this part of the
forest.

He should have turned back, he knew. And he said it, I
must turn back. She was not lost, he was sure. But she
was not going to the adamah, either. The thought of the
work not completed, the unfinished hedge, held him. I will

go a little way; and if I don't find her, I will turn back. There was a spray of the young leaves snapped off and thrown down: for no reason that he could tell. Once, she had circled back and Adam, following with relief, set his face towards the adamah again. If Elohim came, he would tell him, I delayed in the forest a little while, but not long; for Ishah's sake, to be with her. And he thought that Elohim had himself made Ishah to be with Adam; Adam with Ishah: and the tracks swerved aside again through a clearing in the trees.

There, in the open suddenly bright with sunshine, she had taken a whole branch and dragged it down to the midst of the clearing.

Adam knew, then, that she meant him to follow.

The way of the branch along the ground pointed where she had gone. Intent upon the tracks he had given himself no pause to look about him, sensing the direction: now he was so far into the forest it would be as well to go to the adamah this way as by another. But passing among closer trees on rising ground, as the tracks led him on, he knew the place: the ferns growing steeply at his left hand, masking the dell, where the narrow pathway went down to the tree of knowledge. Even before Ishah answered his call, close at hand, he knew that she was within the dell itself.

His first thought was to go to her.

He thrust through the ferns, his feet on the path down, and the cool of the dell flowed back to him in a quiet; and his footsteps slowed, and stopped altogether. He opened his mouth to call her and the thought came to him, The presence of the Lord God is with her.

Because the place was forbidden them; she knew; she would not have gone down of herself.

He went on down more slowly, then, softly, wary of the

brightness. But there was none: only the cool and the half-light. He entered the dell uncertainly and at first did not see her, turning his head this way and that to look.

And then he saw her: and was still.

She was standing by the moss mound, her pale shape there as the white lily by some green pool, his darling, with her hair unbound. And it was like the hurt in his side the day that she was made: the rush of tenderness within him, that lifted his heart to his throat, and choked him. Her face was turned aside, perfectly still, as some forest creature ware of a sound. And yet more beautiful than any creature of earth or air: the last and loveliest thing God made. He said, Ishah, and she turned.

In heaven itself he could imagine none more to be desired; nor any place more blessed than where her feet walked, bringing her to him, the dell a mist of late sunbeams, a place of dreams about her: the smell of her hair remembered, and the littleness of her captive hands—trembling: he felt them tremble, and held them.

—Ishah, he said, and she said, I have something to tell you.

But her eyes fled his own. Not her hands only, but her whole being trembled with some inward excitement, something held secret to amaze him. It was Igwana, he knew: how she had seen the dragon down by the river. He was going to say it; and held his tongue because it would spoil her pleasure. He let her go and she moved restlessly, not looking at him, moving a little way apart, and stopping again. And he thought of the young hinds grazing.

—I have been looking at the tree, she said.

Its shadow lay across her, the dark mass of the leaves here and there speckled with light still. Almost, he had forgotten the tree. He should go from this place, he knew. All through the forest until he found her he had put off his weariness but now, when he stood still, when he leaned down to sit, and lay back against the soft mound of moss, his hands behind his head to watch her, it was as if he lacked the strength so much as to rise again.   And he thought, if the thing displeased Elohim, he would not have sent the woman to go through the forest before Adam.   He closed his eyes, but not for weariness: only so that opening them he might see her there still.   Blood of my blood, he said.   Flesh of my flesh.   And she said, I have been looking at the tree.

It was too late to return to the adamah now.   There would be no light to work by.   And he thought, It is too late; watching her.

—And the fruit of it, she said: is it true that we cannot eat the fruit?   Have you seen it, Adam?—have you seen how tender-skinned and ripe it is?

And then she said, I am sure it is good for food.

—Ishah, Adam said.

He stretched out his hand open for hers, to call her back. Don't be foolish.   Come, let us go.   I know where there is a fruit as yellow and ripe as this . . .   But he did not rise. The thought of the fruit brought his thirst back again, worse than before.   Shall we eat of the forbidden fruit—and die?

He wanted her to laugh, to run and catch hold of his hands, lending her quick strength to his tiredness for the long climb up to the shelter.   But she came slowly.

—You call me foolish, she said.   But we have both been foolish; and more than you know.   We will not die if we eat of the tree.   Do you know why it is called the tree of knowledge?   Because its fruit will make us wise, Adam— wise to know all things!   Igwana himself has told me.

—It is true?   But he did not think it was true.   He caught her wrist, so slender his fingers quite encircled it; touched the sweet curve of her arm.

—It is true, Adam! In the day that we eat the fruit we shall be as the angels.

He held the pale loveliness of her face small between his two hands, infinitely precious to him. As the angels! she said; and he said, What have the angels, that I lack?

—Knowledge! And she drew back with a small fierce movement away from him. They can tell good and evil, they are wise—oh, Adam! Will you be content for ever, to have no more understanding than the beasts? But I am not content for you!

Adam, watching her swift, impatient movements, wanted to smile; and could not; held from smiling by the uncertain truth of her words. She spoke rapidly, urgently; it was as if he were carried away on the stream of her words; no longer listening, but watching her, the movement of her slender shoulders, and her bright hair tossed back. Has Elohim made anything more perfect than this?

It was the movement that gave him warning: the sudden ducking of her bright head in under the tree, her outstretched arm pale among the dark leaves: and he sprang up.

—*Ishah—!*

But he was too late. He caught at her hand, loosening the fruit from her fingers. But she let it go willingly and gave it to him, and slipped away; and he saw that she held another to her mouth.

A moment: and the soft ripple of her laughter came back to him.

—Didn't I tell you? she said. It is sweeter than the honey-comb! Throw yours away then, if you want to. But as for me, Adam, do you still not believe that my eyes will be opened?

And she stood laughing, but softly: fairer than the lily, than the beauty of lilies in the dusk, his darling with her hair unbound—as God made her. Do you still not believe it, Adam, my Adam?

And the thought came to him that God had not made the thing so fair to destroy it, and Adam with her. Not Adam, but God made them one flesh. And he bit through the yellow skin of the fruit in his hand.

And it was as she had said, sweeter than honey and the honeycomb.

17

The Shadow of Death

THEY were naked.

He knew his own nakedness as he stood, and lifting his face, saw Ishah's eyes upon him. In the same moment she turned and fled from the dell.

He might have turned and followed her. But he sat with the yellow fruit in his hand, naked against the grass mound with his knees hunched, his beard on his chest. A trickle of the fruit sap trailed down stickily over his wrist and formed a drop. He looked at the fruit, not seeing it, seeing her image there in naked flight, her face with all the laughter gone out of it.

Even the sound of her was gone.

If she had called him, he would have followed and found her: if she had made so much as a sign or a gesture. And he thought, Let her go, then. The sap on his wrist was sticky, and he wiped his wrist on the grass. In his mouth it had for a little eased his thirst, but now it was worse than before, with a bitter taste.

And he thought it was well with the woman, because she had drunk her fill at the than, and rested, and afterwards had come up here walking at her ease. But as for Adam, he had neither drunk nor rested from the hill pastures to the dell for her sake. Beside the river she had not waited for his coming, and in the dell she fled from him—it was as though she fled from him—caring nothing for his weariness.

He was angry, then. The fruit he had tasted was gall in his mouth. The thirst tormented him, and he bit into the fruit again more deeply for the first sweetness of it, and got up, and went to the tree for another—one more. And he said, Seeing I have tasted of the tree.

—What is it to me, whether I eat one fruit or two?

He ate seven before his thirst was satisfied. Twice he stopped still to listen: and once turned his head to look behind him. Above the high banks the forest ringed the dell with darkness, as it were full of eyes that watched him. And he suddenly snatched up a stone in his hand and flung it high over the bank.

He heard it strike among branches, and then crash down in the ferns.

But nothing moved there.

Once, he thought Ishah had returned. He imagined she crept silently, with suppressed laughter, to surprise him. But when he looked, the dell was empty.

Not empty: peopled with shadows like living things, creeping closer little by little, moment by moment near; hidden when he looked; watching him all the time.

He left the dell half running, not looking back, in haste from the naked half-light for the refuge of the trees, for the closer darkness to cover him, to lose himself in it safe and be as one with the night and the forest creatures. But even the darkness was alien. He ran wildly, hurting himself among the waiting trees, spewing out the bitter aftertaste of the fruit, but he could not spew it out, it clung in his mouth. There seemed no end to the forest, no way out that he could find or remember: he could find no pathway through the tangled underwoods. The place was quiet for his stumbling. He fell, and there was no sound at all: only the listening for him; the listening and the waiting. And then, when he would have cried out aloud for Elohim the gall rose in his throat and choked him, and he lay as one dead.

And this was death, the absence of God: to be alone in the dark, and afraid.

It was the thought of the shelter that drew him to his feet at last: the shelter and the light and warmth of the fire, and the river behind to take away the taste and wash his mouth clean. Ishah would be there already, he knew. And he saw her face again in imagination, not as he had seen it when she fled, but smiling, laughing softly, her little face uplifted to his own, saying Adam, my Adam. Perhaps she would be restless for him to come, walking this way and that— towards the river, perhaps. He wondered if her mouth was bitter as his own.

He found the gate at last by its path of pallor, a little light let through: the hewn stakes sideways as he had himself made them, one above another barred against the moon, the moonlight over the adamah, silver in a mist, and one bright star low down. Then he was over the gate, and it was not a star, it was the small fire twinkling before the shelter.

She was there. As he drew nearer he saw her throw a piece of wood on the fire, and the sparks fly upwards. The light flared an instant to show the side of her face, and her arm outstretched.

It showed Igwana there also, the firelight glinting on his scales. Because of the dragon, Adam went up between the standing corn and the river. He approached the shelter from behind and hung back in the shadows. He could see the hinder part of the dragon only, the hind talons and the tapering thickness of the tail curled aside, the scales in the firelight glowing like live embers.

—When I saw him, I was afraid . . .

It was the woman's voice.

—I know now what an evil thing it is—to fear! And yet why should I fear the leopard? who has been with us from the beginning.

The dragon answered her. Because your eyes are opened: nor can the thing be hidden from you any longer. For if the leopard turn on you, tooth and claw, how will you resist him? Or who shall save you? Seeing that he is able to tear you, as you tear the flesh of the ripe fruit. Your bones are like brittle sticks to him; like the snapping of deadwood.

—If it be so, I do well to fear him. And not the leopard only, but the lion, ch'hora—and Behemoth! And she said, Shall I fear Behemoth? who has carried me from place to place, yes, and followed me like s'gala wherever I led him . . . ? Shall we not rule over the beasts of the field?

—Not by your lesser strength, but by your greater wisdom, you shall rule over them: by reason of the fire you kindle, and your high hedges. The axe you have already. But I tell you, in the day of your weakness, even the stones shall fight for you.

—What does this mean, Even the stones . . . ?

—Ask your husband, the dragon said, and she said, Adam? And then Igwana said, Even Adam, who is standing close by us. Nevertheless, for his nakedness he will not come to the light while I remain . . .

She said again, Adam? The firelight sparkled down the scales in changing hues as the dragon withdrew. He looked back and for a long moment surveyed the shadows where the man stood. Then, with his leisurely stride, he moved beyond the circle of light into the mist. Adam watched him go: the moonlight on the adamah, and Ishah's voice called in question, Adam?

—Adam . . .

—I am here.

Ishah was within the shelter. He heard her move. But she did not come out. Then she said, Why don't you come?

—Am I Behemoth? Adam said: to be led by the nose after you. Or s'gala, that I must trot at your heel?

She came out to him, then. She touched his hands, glancing up at his face, and ran to fetch water from the than for him to drink. She set fruit beside him, and shelled the corn meal, and made a place soft in the shelter for him to rest his head. But he sat where he was against the centre post, with his face towards the fire.

—Is it because I didn't wait for you, she said, that you are angry, Adam?

She said, Tell me.

Though he was no longer angry, neither would he tell her. He heard her sigh, as she lay down behind him; the rustle of dry reeds, and then still. He wanted to turn and look on her face again. He wanted to kneel, and touch her hair, and speak her name for love of her. But he kept his face to the fire.

Sitting there, he thought of Igwana, and what the dragon had said about the weakness of man, The stones shall fight for you. And he had said, Ask your husband.

Because Adam in the dell had taken a stone to fight for him, flinging it from his hand to search the darkness.

Igwana had been with him, then. All the time. Even in the dell.

And he knew then why it was that Igwana had wings, and no longer flew; why he knew the angels by name, and was wise, and answered no call; why the dragon's scaled spine was bruised and purple, and he limped on one foot. And why he was never to be seen when the presence of the Lord God was close in the garden.

Adam lifted his eyes a little, wearily, looking at the misty darkness beyond the fire. He ate a little of the corn meal. And then presently, when he would have turned and gone in to Ishah, he saw that she was asleep.

He might have wakened her, whispering her name, Ishah, beloved ... But for a little while longer he sat there. The fire grew smaller, the misty shadows drawing in. He took up the fruit which she had set beside him, and it was yellow: the same which she had carried in her hand when she fled from the dell.

He drew back his arm and hurled it with all his strength, far out over the adamah.

Then he turned back into the shelter, to drown himself in the forgetfulness of sleep.

18

The Dragon's Disciples

THE DAY was as other days, the morning clear and bright
with the renewal of familiar things: freshness in the air and
the dewfresh birdsong, the riverrunning, and the live smell
of the earth. To Adam, turning his eyes towards the forest
in the moment of waking, it was as though he had dreamed
an evil dream. Far down the gate made a gap in the hedge-
line through which the forest showed a sunlit bower, dwelling place of the parakeet, and the chattering bush-tail.

Ishah was not in the shelter when he woke. Half in
sleep with the uncertain stirrings of desire he looked for her,
but she had risen already and gone out. To the river, perhaps; she was nowhere about the adamah. Looking out
across the level brown earth, Adam marvelled that the corn
they had sown should have started so soon to spring up. It
showed as a patch of yellow: yet not the corn—it was not
the corn, it was the yellow fruit.

He turned back quickly, thinking of Ishah, palm down to
her sleeping place, wondering where she was. There was
no warmth of her, she had been gone a long while; and he
thought doubtless to the river. And he thought he would
go there also, and refresh himself from sleeping as at other
times before. Then he saw the axe lying there, and thought
he would take it with him, and bring kindling wood. And
then he looked to the fire, the ashes and the kindling there

to see if more was needed and the fruit was there yellow on the adamah. Because the adamah was everywhere level and brown, the smooth yellow ball of the fruit caught the sunlight and drew his eyes, compelling him to look. And it seemed to him, half standing, half kneeling in the mouth of the shelter, it seemed to grow larger and brighter, rounder and more yellow, until it stood out like the sun itself for all the garden to see.

He ran out naked as he was and set his heel on it—a little, round, yellow fruit no bigger than his clenched hand. It was shrivelled a little, with lying exposed to the sun. He stamped his bare heel down once, and again, smashing and crushing the soft split mass of it into the brownsoil, and a long white worm came wriggling urgently out of the pulp.

Ishah laughed when he told her.

She came down from the direction of the upper forest, her hair garlanded with anemones, climbing the gate awkwardly for the sheaf of great fronds she held, coming down the edge of the adamah with the fronds held against her for a covering. He told her, and she laughed, and kissed him with her mouth because he was troubled for the sake of a worm and there were worms everywhere in the adamah, they had turned up any number with the soil. And she laughed and gave him one of the green fronds to cover himself and turned to go out again, and he said, Ishah, stay with me.

—I am going for meat, she said: come with me ... Or stay; and I will fetch some for you.

But he went with her, drawing a frond about him for a girdle, as she had done, binding it with a liana. The fronds were stiff and cumbersome to walk with, and difficult to manage, slowing their strides to a careful, ponderous walking

—like Behemoth! she said. He would have stayed at the corn to eat, but she drew him on, wanting to go farther down to the fruit trees; and it was true, fruit was better than corn in the heat of the morning. But he hesitated a moment longer, looking at the high sun.

—What of the adamah?

But she drew him on by the arm. It is the Sabbath! She laughed, so that he was unsure. He might have gone back and numbered the stones, but he went on with her, walking beside the thán again, down past the riverfalls, where she had gone in after the kid that day. She was just as high as his eyes, walking beside him.

—We will eat first, she said. And afterwards we will see to the work.

Her hair was as new honey, or as the ripe corn, starred with anemones, scarlet and white, gathered at the nape of her neck for coolness, softest golden downward plume between her shoulder blades. She frowned as she walked, impatient with the heavy fronds' banging against her knees. The frown made a tiny crease between her brows.

—I wish we had the beauty of scales to cover us, she said: like Igwana!

If she had wished for the sun or the moon, he would have given them her.

—I will make you scales, he said.

They were not as Igwana's. And yet the five-tongued leaves strung overlapping, green upon green, had somewhat the appearance of scales: enough to make Ishah clap her hands with delight. Adam made the first, and then after-wards they worked together, choosing the fig leaves for their pleasing shape, and threading them with strands of lianas as the woman joined her garlands. They made girdles for themselves, and hung the green scales from them, strand by strand, working side by side through the long afternoon, holding up the strands to compare them and laughing, together through the long afternoon between forest and river, sunshine and shadow; sometimes Ishah ran to fetch leaves, calling to show him, mingling her cries with the birdsong, her laughter with the rippling river, and it was as if the afternoon was golden for them, and everything made for their pleasure alone: the sun in the sky to warm them, the thán to refresh, the grasses made soft and pleasant for their feet, and everything full of delight, carefree. The leaf-decked girdles were better than the fronds, lighter and more free. Ishah ran and turned, swirling the strands rustling, and clapped her hands, and threw back her head to laugh again, and his heart went out to her. She ran under the trees snatching down a soft fruit as she passed to fling it back to him, and it struck him on the shoulder and ran down; and she laughed and fled over the grass for no purpose but that he should pursue and catch her, and snatch her up lightly with her rustling apron of leaves in his arms, and carry her down into the grass to kiss the softness of her hair, and her mouth, and she said, Am I an angel, Adam? And he said, You are all angels to me. And then when she would have risen again he forced her wrists down, and she resisted him, and he held her there. Her eyes widened in surprise at the hurt and her own helplessness and then, twisting her head, she sank her teeth into the flesh of his arm so that he let go with a cry, and she wriggled out of his grasp and sprang up.

She outran him to the river's edge, and when he would have caught her again, turned and slipped her hand in his. She laid her head against his shoulder. I am too tired to run farther. What shall we do, Adam? Shall we go and find other fruit?

Some of the green figs they had eaten while gathering the leaves, but not many; it was not good to eat too many. Her face was towards the forest, and he said, Not from the dell.

She looked surprised. No; here beside the thán. There are many trees here. There are only two in the dell.

—Two, Adam said.

He had thought there was one. But he remembered, then when she said it; when he followed her down the riverside again, following the swing and rustle of her rapid stride, under the speckled shade, the fruit trees about them: he remembered that there was in truth a second tree in the dell beside the tree of knowledge. But he did not want to remember the dell, and swung himself up into the nearest tree, calling out to her to catch the fruit when he threw it down.

Afterwards, they crossed over the river shallows, wading. He climbed first on to the bank, and turned to help her: and her fingers caught at his arm, painfully tense.

—Adam . . .

The leopard was there. He did not see it at first, because it was at a little height above the ground, lying along a branch among the first trees that screened the swamp. It had turned its head at their approach, and regarded them, amber-eyed. For a moment Adam stood uncertain, detained by the woman's anxious hold on his arm. Then, gently freeing himself, he stooped to select a smooth and heavy stone from the shallow river bed.

In the same moment the leopard sprang down and went bounding away into the swamp.

They went on, not speaking, occupied with their separate thoughts, following the bank upstream in the sun. Their thighs brushed as they walked, and he was going to speak to her again, to ask her of the leopard; but seeing her face remote from him, her thoughts turned inwards, said nothing. Presently, tiring of the stone's heaviness in his hand, he hurled it into the thán; and ran to watch the splash it made. Ishah came beside him, hand on his shoulder. They found other, smaller stones and lingered on the bank, throwing them in; watching the spurt of water, leaping up and falling back in widening ripples. They thought they saw Leviathan there, deep down; or it might have been their own combined shadow, leaning together over the water. They saw the blue kingfisher and called him to them; but for the stones in their hands he would not come; and they did not care if he came or not. And then, seeing that he would not, Adam pitched a stone to put him to flight: watching the swift blue streak over the water. The sun was hot on their shoulders; too hot; and presently Ishah let fall her apron of leaves and slipped into the stream, gliding down under the surface half way to the far bank. He saw her head break the surface. She shook her hair back, and he went in after her, twisting and turning down underwater, opening his eyes to a strange and green world, surfacing again for breath, swimming towards the woman where she turned her head to watch for him. They swam until they grew tired and climbed out on the farther bank to shake themselves and lie in the sun. It was cooler now, with the first suggestion of a breeze, the first winds of evening moving through the garden. Adam lay still, as in sleep, drowsy with the sun and with swimming; aware of her nakedness beautiful on the bank beside him, the sunshine on her skin, bare of the covering leaves now, heel and thigh, and the hollow of her back.

He wondered if she was angry, for her silence; or if she slept, cheek on the white curve of her arm. But when he glanced secretly at her, he saw that she watched him covertly from under lowered lashes. Her mouth trembled to a smile, half smiling; and she turned her face away. He reached out an arm to claim her, drawing her to him, and she drew away. He caught hold of her wrists and forced them down, and she resisted him, and he held her. Her eyes went to the mark on his arm, where her teeth had marked it, but she did not move. She lifted her eyes in the shadow of his face, and the wind ruffled her wet hair.

—Ishah . . .

It was then that he heard on the wind the voice of the Lord God calling, and all at once she was weeping and saying Adam what have we done, what have we done.

19

The Wages of Sin

HE HAD never seen her weeping. He crouched half kneeling in an agony of indecision, naked on the open bank and the voice of the Lord God was approaching through the garden. She wrenched away from him, casting about in blind haste for the leaf girdles to cover herself, and they were on the other side of the river, but she went on looking for them. He left her there and fled into the forest.

A little way; not far. He ran into the trees, and was unsure. He thought the voice was behind in the riverfields: but it was in the forest.

—Adam!

He stood among ferns, his heart beating. The echo went to and fro, Adam! Adam! into the forest. He ran, and stopped: turned, and ran, and turned again: and he seemed to run towards the sound whichever way he turned.

—Adam!

And again—Adam! on the wind, carried on the air through the open glades, down the paths, in the thickets—Adam!—Adam! all about him everywhere, near and far, and he turned running and it seemed as if the very trees shouted and called —Adam!—Adam!—Adam! to betray him, nowhere a refuge, to run to, to hide him, until it seemed as if the whole length and breadth of the forest rang with his name—Adam!—Adam! —ADAM!

And he stood still. The echoes died away, and it was quiet again: only his heart beating.

—Where are you?

He answered without raising his eyes, his head bowed. I heard your voice in the garden . . .

—And I was afraid, because I was naked . . .

And he said, I hid myself.

He stood in the presence of the Lord God. The forest grasses at his feet were afire with a brilliance of radiant light, burning as green and golden flames. He did not lift his eyes.

—Who told you that you were naked?

But he could not answer.

—Have you eaten of the tree, of which I commanded you that you should not eat?

—I did eat, Adam said.

And it seemed to him beyond belief, that he could have done it. He saw himself in the dell again, naked, but they had not known they were naked, and Ishah with the fruit in her hand, one in each hand; which he had taken and eaten freely, it was true, as if he had forgotten the commandment.

But he knew that he had not forgotten it, and that it was for Ishah's sake, not his own; because the Lord God had made her fair, and of Adam one flesh, so that his heart went out to her and he loved her, and did not care.

—The woman whom you gave to be with me, Adam said: she gave me the fruit, and I ate it.

—Call her to me, the Lord God said.

Adam called her by name. She was not far away. She had hidden as he had, among the trees. He heard her footsteps approach but the brightness compelled his eyes down; he did not see her. He heard the voice of the Lord God say, Ishah, what is this that you have done? And she said, the dragon beguiled me, and I ate the fruit.

—Where is the dragon? the Lord God said.
But they could not say.

—Adam . . . ?
The woman's voice, soft in the darkness. He lifted his
face, but he could see nothing: only a faint glimmer of light
which remained, above the trees.
—I am here.
He heard her move, and made his way forward to meet
her; their hands touched, and clung.
They did not speak until they had come up out of the
forest, and climbed the gate to the open adamah, the moonlight pale on her hair at his shoulder. And then she said,
Adam, what will become of us? But he could not tell her.
—How shall we escape death? she said: seeing we have
sinned against God; even the Lord God who made us.
She wept, and for a little way he comforted her, his arm
about her shoulder, speaking to her gently. It is Elohim,
Ishah: we must let him judge. Surely the time for tears is
past; whatever we have done is known now: we have no
need to run from the presence of the Lord God any more.
Let us go back to the shelter openly, and wait for him there.
And he said, It may be he will have mercy on us even now,
to prolong our days.
She clung to him. Is it possible?
But he could not say that it was possible.

The light of their fire brought Igwana out of the shadow
of the forest a little before morning, under the bar of the gate,
down by the shadow of the hedge. He drew close, and
warmed himself as before. Why does the woman weep?
And he said, Has God made her weep? I heard his voice
in the forest, as it were in anger.

And then he said to the woman, Won't you tell me what God has said, to make you sorrowful?

—Let her be, Adam said. What have we to do with you? If you hadn't deceived us with lies, we should not have sinned against God; nor would there be any sorrow or tears.

The dragon was still.

—Take care, Adam. Watch your tongue when you speak to me. Do you know who I am? Be very careful you do not make me angry.

And he said, Look at me, Adam.

Unwillingly, Adam turned his head. The amber eyes drew his gaze, compelling his to look. He shivered, and would have looked away, and could not. In the darkness the dragon's eyes glowed with the firelight, the red and flickering embers. Are you not afraid, Adam? Do you know the power I have over you?

He moved in a little closer, his eyes on the man's face, and Adam would have moved back; and could not.

—I cannot help being afraid, he said. But I fear God more. For unless the Lord God gives it you, you have no power over me to harm me: neither you, nor the beasts of the field.

—Do you speak to me, Igwana said, of lies? But his eyes were hooded now, their smouldering fires dimmed: and he lowered his head to rest it. Show me, show me when I have lied to you. Are not your eyes opened, even as I promised the woman? Ah, see now the ingratitude of man. For I had pity on your ignorance. What God withheld I gave you freely: even of the tree of the knowledge of good and evil, so that you would be wise, even as I am wise.

Adam took a faggot of wood and threw it on the fire, so

that the flames leaped up again. In the greater light the dragon seemed to diminish, shrinking back with the shadows.

—The fruit was not yours to give, Adam said, but Elohim's. Have you any good thing to give us?

For a long moment, the dragon regarded him unwaveringly, his scaled head rested between his talons.

—Do you retain your integrity? Or do you still hope in God? What is the use; seeing he goes about to kill you, and nothing you do pleases him. Don't you see that his ways are too hard for you: he has set pitfalls to make your feet stumble, more than flesh and blood is able to overcome. Even the angels have not been tried as you have. But consider for a moment: look about you. Are there not pleasures enough to satisfy you in this delightful garden?—they are yours for the taking, Adam. Do you lift your eyes and dream of another heaven—afar and hereafter? Oh, Adam . . . foolish Adam! Are not your eyes opened, as mine are opened? We are of one spirit, you and I; our heaven is here, is now, even the wide earth, to possess it for our own. Follow me now, and do you know what I will give you? I will give you the fruit of the second tree in the dell, which is the tree of life, and you shall live for ever.

And he said, You, and the woman with you . . .

—Adam.
—I hear you, Adam said.

He lifted his eyes and saw the dragon start up, half turned in a moment too late to run, and then sink back to the earth in the dazzling radiance of the presence of the Lord God.

20

The Mercy of God

WHO IS THIS that disannuls my judgment? who makes my word of no effect, and deceives my own.

The glory of the Lord God shone full on Igwana. In the blinding radiance of light the dragon seemed to writhe and shrivel, as a green leaf in the midst of fire.

—Because you have done this, the Lord God said, you are cursed above all cattle, and above every beast of the field.

As a leaf among flames the dragon curled and twisted, curved in a bow of agony, tail tip to head: flung out, and curled again: flung and curled. His scales like dead leaves rattled together, sere and brittle and then, abruptly, split open down the length of his underbelly as a husk of corn.

—Upon your belly shall you go, and dust shall you eat all the days of your life.

Out of the husk sloughed off, there came sliding a new creature, with the head of Igwana and a new brightness of scales gleaming, banded with colours: yet wingless, sliding upon its belly.

—And I will put enmity between you and the woman, the Lord God said: and between your seed and her seed; he shall bruise your head, and you shall bruise his heel.

The creature moved as water flowing, down beside the shelter of leaves, slithering into the grass there towards the river, and was gone under the low mist.

Within the shelter, the woman suddenly covered her face. She crouched there, shaking.

—I will greatly multiply your sorrow and your conception, the Lord God said: in sorrow you shall bring forth children; and your desire shall be to your husband, and he shall rule over you.

And he said, Adam . . .

The man lay with his face to the earth. It was as if the noonday sun stood close over him: and he was naked.

—Because you have listened to the voice of your wife, the Lord God said, and have eaten of the tree, of which I commanded you, saying, You shall not eat of it: cursed is the ground for your sake. In sorrow you shall eat of it all the days of your life. And it shall bring forth thorns and thistles to you; and you shall eat the herb of the field. In the sweat of your face, you shall eat bread.

And he said, Behold, the man is become as one of us, to know good and evil.

—Now therefore, lest you stretch out your hand, and take the fruit of the tree of life also, and live forever in the flesh with sorrow, you shall go forth from the garden to till the ground from which you were taken, until you return to the earth; for out of it you were taken. For you are dust, and to dust you shall return.

—Lord God, Adam said: will you send us away, naked as we are?

—Lift up your eyes towards the river. And I will show you, what you must do.

Because of the morning mist there, Adam could at first see nothing. It was the sound, as of cattle over beyond the stream, that drew him down to the bank: the stamping of hooves, and the clink of horn on horn. Ishah came fearfully beside him, to see.

—It is b'hemah, she said.

But it was the red deer. They saw them through a thinning of the mist, two harts of the red deer which strained together on the far bank, their heads lowered one against the other, with their antlers entangled. Before the mist closed again, they saw the one on the left hand slip and fall, pulling the other down with it.

—Come, let us go over, Adam said.

He drew Ishah after him, down beside the river at a trot, wary of the margin that was half hidden; hurrying down below the sound of the falls, where they could cross safely. The shallows were fresh and cold at this hour, breathing mist. Upstream past the falls again on the far bank they ran to warm themselves.

They found the two harts still as they had fallen, their heads curiously twisted upwards to the sky, fastened together by the thicket of antlers. Adam, kneeling swiftly to free them, set a hand on each: and then, gradually, let go.

—What is it? Ishah said.

The flesh under Adam's hand was warm and still. Under the mass of antlers the eyes stared sightless up at him. He set his palm over the open nostrils; and there was nothing. What is it? Ishah asked him: are they asleep? And he told her, there is no breath in them.

—They are dead, Ishah, dead.

It was a moment before she understood. And then, with a slow awakening of pity she looked at the beautiful creatures as they lay, and bent to touch them with a wondering gentleness. Ah, Adam . . . ! I know that we have deserved to die . . .

And she said, But how have these sinned? Or what evil

have they done, that Elohim has cut them off in their strength?

It was not until they had returned to the adamah, to the shelter of leaves there, when Adam saw the dragon's husk lying beside the ashes of the fire, that he could answer her question.

—Surely the harts are slain for us, Ishah: to cover our nakedness.

He went inside the shelter to choose an axe head. He had made many, flaking them sharp with quick blows with a hammer stone, spoiling more flints than he finished; but there were seven made perfect. He chose two, trying the edges with his thumb, and took them in his hand without the hafts. There was no need for the hafts. Ishah was standing by the ashes of the fire. He opened his mouth to speak: and said nothing. Seeing her there standing, waiting, he was aware of the change in her.

Always, when she stood idle there was a restlessness about her, a watchfulness of her blue eyes, alert as some forest creature, her bright head tossed, heel turning, her fingers plucking at some leaf or stem. Now she stood in a dull quiet, her hands hanging, downcast. And he was afraid. The thought came to him that it was not Ishah the Lord God had cursed, saying, You shall go forth from the garden. Not Ishah; but Adam only.

She said, It isn't like the garden, is it?—this place you were taken from.

But there was no remembrance of it he could bring to mind: only that he had stood once, one day at noon, at the farthest limit of the garden, and had looked out at the wilderness beyond: the place of stones and rough pasture, green and brown and grey, and the far mountains. And he told her, where the trees were few and far between, a desert of shadeless knolls and terraces, a thirsty land.

He did not look at her when he told her. He looked across the adamah, where he had sown the seeds of corn which would sometime grow tall, and cover the adamah from hedge to hedge with the mass of their swaying golden crests, very beautiful in the sunshine; but he would not see it. He said aloud, In a little while, I must go away from here: the mouth of the Lord God has spoken it.

—So be it. But as for you, Ishah ... I don't know: whether he will let you stay ...

He did not look at her. He sensed that she came closer, moved beside him, but kept his eyes fixed on the adamah, looking towards the lower forest: the hedge there, and the gate which he had made in the hedge. And he thought, Has God made the trees grow there for no purpose?

If we had only overcome ... If we had only been faithful, obedient to Elohim, and had withheld our hands from the forbidden tree: Elohim would have given us the fruit freely to eat. And he knew it, then. Even the fruit of the tree of life.

—Wherever you go, Ishah said: I will go. And where you die, I will die with you.

He turned to her then, and tried to speak; and there were no words, to tell her. And he suddenly laughed, and she said, Does Adam laugh?

—Seeing the Lord God's hand is stretched out against you—to curse the very ground for your sake! Aren't you being driven out of the garden, cut off from everything that is pleasant and delightful?

—Yet I live, Adam said.

She spread her hands in mute protest; and dropped them listlessly. *Live.* What is your life to be? in a strange land, among thorns and thistles; in some desert place and far from every good thing. I would rather die like the harts, here in the garden! And she said what is your life.

—You are my life, Ishah.

But she continued to stare at the ground.

—My *eve*, he said: my life . . .

He took the axe heads in his hand and went down beside the river again. Because of the tumult of the falls he did not hear her feet running until she was close at his heels. Then he turned and she was in his arms, the soft sheen of her hair at his throat.

—Ishah . . .

—*Eve*, she said.

And he said, Eve.

21

Exile

THEY skinned the deer where they lay, and the carcases heaped about with deadwood, and set it ablaze. They cleaned the skins in the thán, and afterwards staked them out on the adamah in the sun to dry, working and bending them to keep them supple.

Afterwards, the woman went early to sleep, returning to the shelter again as soon as they had eaten and refreshed themselves, to stretch herself out on the dry rushes with a sigh, her cheek on her arm, her face towards the man's coming. But was asleep before he came in.

Adam made no fire by the shelter that night. The air was warm still from the day; there was no wind. Across the river he could see that other fire still burning, sending its sparks straight upwards in the dusk, ascending: among the stars, it seemed, higher far than the deer in their lives had ever dreamed of leaping. Within the shelter the woman Eve lay sleeping. He could hear, if he listened for it, the slow rise and fall of her sleeping breath. The night was marvellously still. For a long time he sat and watched, first the sparks, and then the last flames below them; the brighter for the on-coming darkness. And then afterwards by moonlight, the smoke that climbed ever higher and more high, up and up until it seemed to enter heaven itself. And it seemed to him as if the deer, by reason of their death on the earth, might somehow have returned to him who made them.

Until the skins were dried they clothed themselves with leaves as before, setting them aside only when they swam in the thán to cool themselves, or lay in the shelter at night to sleep. During the days they busied themselves about the adamah; no longer tilling the ground there, but gathering the river corn seed in, which they would carry with them to sow again in the new land outside the garden; binding on new hafts to the axe heads, and hammering new blades of flints ready. They discovered a use for the dragonskin husk, to make pouches to carry the corn; making a needle of a bone splinter pierced through, with which to sew them, joining two pieces together for each. It was in the same manner afterwards, when the deerskins were dried out, that they made coats for themselves, and left off the aprons of leaves altogether.

It was very hot and still. The face of the adamah quivered in a rising haze under the sun, breathless. The hedges were silent, empty of birds now, bare of life, their green leaves faded to a dead and brittle brown. Under the hedgerows the edge of sun and shadow was sharp as the axe blade. Only the forest beyond, the high and living green, showed a promise of cool. But neither the man nor Eve went down.

They lay just inside the shelter, lacking the will even to walk as far as the thán again. They had been twice already to swim, to cool their flesh under the riverfall for the reviving splash and spray of it; but each time returning they were sweating before they reached the shelter again.

Now that the coats of skin were made, there was nothing to delay their going from the garden: but neither of them

spoke of it. The woman had found a green frond cool with
sap, and held it against her cheek: Eve—but he did not look
at her. There was nothing to delay their going. The
thought unspoken was a dividing hedge between them.
Perhaps because her random gaze was towards the pouches
of the dragonskin, filled swollen with corn seed and set in
shade against the centre post, Eve said, What do you think . . .

—Where did Igwana go? after he was changed . . .

But he could not tell her. God knows.

She said meekly, It is true, the Lord God knows all things.

He was rebuked by her meekness, while yet moved by it:
half willing to answer her softly, with gentleness, a tender
word to reach through to her; half driven by the perversity
of his mood to humble her more.

—Weren't you here with me, he said, when Igwana was
sent away? Did he say anything to me? Or do you think
the Lord God has spoken privately in my ear at some time.

She said, I cannot tell; sometimes the Lord God makes
things known to you without speaking. Didn't he show you
how to use these skins, with which we are now clothed?

It was true; but he was angrier for the truth of it. Why
must you trouble me with your questions? Shall I not sleep?

—I will put my hand over my mouth, Eve said.

He closed his eyes to sleep; and for the heat, could not.
He lay on his face, separate from her, his eyes pressed against
his forearm for the greater darkness, willing himself to sleep,
to plunge himself into a depth of sleep, to some calm there
deep under the present turmoil of his thoughts, some escape
from the knowledge that stood at the gate of his mind, go
forth from the garden, go forth from the garden, turning back
within himself; shifting and turning again restlessly until
he opened his eyes awake suddenly to the pattern of the leaves
woven together under the roof darkened and stained with the

woodsmoke and the voice of the Lord God sounding out of the midst of the heavens.

The sound filled the bowl of the sky with anger: echoings that walked to and fro on the earth and shook its foundations —Adam, snatching up axe and pouches, saw Eve's stricken face and caught her wrist to hasten her rising. She was trembling violently and clung to him, crying with words he could not hear. He thrust one of the pouches into her shaking hands and pulled her after him out of the shelter, breaking the corn down headlong through it, running down beside the thán, hampered by the pouches' swing and banging down past the plunging waterfalls running through the spray flung scattered in the rising wind—down by the fruit groves under purple and amber splashing through the delaying shallows past the saplings, the swampland, running through flowering grasses the wind at their backs as the breath of God behind them, they broke through a strangling thicket, the man shouldering a way through, drawing Eve after him; broke through and ran again and then the garden was behind them shaken with the voice of the Lord God Jehovah, every leaf and frond blown wild with the rushing wings of the wind.

Not until they reached the second ridgeline, when the woman stumbled for breath and Adam caught and steadied her, did they look back.

The wind in their faces blurred their last sight of the garden: a line of rich and verdant green, half hidden under gathering clouds, grey and dark, and then suddenly flickering with light; tossing trees and the windflecked river flowing down out of them, far below now; the narrow strip of green herbage that bordered the river, following its twists and turnings through a brown and rock-strewn valley at their feet; the wilderness rising on every side of the garden, climbing in terraced ridges like that on which they stood, flecked with green of the scattered shrubs and single trees; grey with stones, brown with the sandsoil to the bare mountains beyond.

They went on more slowly, in silence, making their way down the far side of the ridge. The wind dropped suddenly and they felt the warmth of the sun again, warm underfoot where there was no shade. And then they were climbing higher once more, and into the wind again. At the third ridge, which was the crest, they looked down on the broad sweep of the land below them: the land through which they must pass.

It lay still under the sun, and glittering silver-white, patterned with the rise and fall of little hills that dwindled away to the far horizons. Far away on their left hand as a flash of silver they saw the river again in its course; and one cluster of tiny trees there where the river divided into two; and divided again as the fingers of the hand spread out, where the sky stood blue at the end of the earth.

For a long moment they stood, and looked at the place. And then Eve, sinking down on a stone, let fall the pouch she carried and covered her face with her hands.

As much as he could, Adam comforted her.

He knelt at her side, so that his shadow was over her, encouraging her with the promise of evening, the cool that must come—presently; quite soon. He spoke of the easier, the downward path in front of them, out of the wind altogether, and cool in the evening. Eve ... rest a little now, and get your strength back. We will stay here until the heat is past ...

And he said, Eve, listen to me ...

—I would rather go back to the garden, she said. I would rather die in the presence of the Lord God, where he is.

Adam said nothing. He shifted a little, making his knees

a pillow for her head, stroking her hair gently. He watched their one shadow creep out and lengthen, slanting over the smaller stones. Because they were under the ridge there was no wind, but below, in the open wilderness, it would be already cooler. He lifted her gently and freed himself, stretching his legs painfully and pulling the deerskin up at his shoulder where it had slipped down. He walked a little way, easing the cramp in his legs, watching her, but she did not move. He climbed the short distance up to the top of the ridge again, breathing the air, the wind blowing strongly in his face again as he came to the crest; thinking of her words, I would rather go back, and the wind in his face blowing his hair about, driving him away. I would rather die in the presence of the Lord God.

Where he is.

Watching him, Eve called out, What is it? And he said, Come and see. And she said, Can you still see the garden?

But they could not, for the ridges in between. They could see no more than the bowl of the hills, where the light flickered still under dark storm clouds, a needle of fire as a white flame sudden between heaven and earth; now on this side, now on that; touching the earth with a blade of flame and gone, here and there about the place where the garden was, on every side of it. Watching it, Adam remembered the tree that had stood among the trees of the forest: how the fire like this, out of the darkened heavens, had struck down and consumed it in a moment of time. He had told the woman of it before; they had stood often beside the same tree charred and blackened on the adamah and he had told her, and she had touched it with wondering fingers. And now, watching her face beside him, he knew that she also remembered.

The wind in her face flecked her cheeks with tears like his

own; or perhaps she wept of herself. But she made no move. If she had said it again, I would rather go back, he would have gone with her, even now. But she said nothing; only stood.

Below the ridges the valley grew indistinct in the gathering dusk, the far hills no longer clear against the sky but remote as shadows, merging one into another, losing distinctness. Only about the bowl of the hills, where the garden was, the light remained.

It was the wings that drove them away at last: the sound of the wings in the valley, hovering, gathering closer and louder, pinion upon pinion, flight upon flight unseen, beating the air to a rushing of storm winds all one way; sounding through the valley until it was as if the voice of the Lord God Jehovah came upon them in the one great hurricane blast that drove them away down over the ridge for shelter.

They went on down, then; gathering up the pouches as they went, picking their way down in the uncertain light, the man and the woman together.

22

The Garden Remembered

By day they might have made their way straight, taking their direction from the place of the sunrise and continuing until its setting behind them; but because they journeyed by night to escape the heat of the day, the sun rose sometimes on their left hand, or on their right. During the day they rested and slept the heat out under shade where they found it: among rocks sometimes, or in hollows scooped under the dunefalls, but more often under the bank of one of the dry and waterless channels that ran everywhere across the land.

The place where the river divided, which they had marked from the ridge as the fingers of the hand spread out, they never found again.

Water of a kind they found under the bed of the dry channels, digging as some creature had digged before them, whose tracks they discovered and lost again on stony ground; and twice among rocks in a living spring, where they drank their fill. One night it rained, and for three days the channels ran with water: brimming, lessening, dwindling, and on the fourth day dry again. For meat, until they came upon the first lone cluster of fruit trees, they had nothing but the corn they carried with them.

They numbered the days as they had always numbered them, by sevens, taking up a small stone each morning until the Sabbath, and leaving the seven behind in the place where they rested that day: but how many Sabbaths they marked in the wilderness, or how many days they were there, they could not afterwards tell. Nor could they tell at any time, looking back, which of the many ridges distant against the sky was the one they had passed over. Nor whether the river, whose banks they reached the third day after one Sabbath, was the same which flowed out of the garden of Eden.

They saw it first at daybreak, climbing all night among rising hills but without hope, they had climbed many hills, and always to find the wilderness at daybreak in front of them the same as behind; yet this day the first light rising at the edge of the sky touched the earth with green again, very far off: the irregular outline of wooded hills, trees, the glitter of water here and there between them, the river, and a white mist rising from it.

Afterwards, though Adam never forgot the moment of it, the first sight of the green hills, it was the woman's face that he chiefly remembered: her small face shadowed by the one lank tress pushed back and fallen again, lustreless; her face streaked with dirt and sand-dust and sweat, the glitter of tears trembling under her eyelids on the brink of disbelief, her lips quivering as if they would spill out the overflow of her heart's gladness in some wild laughter, and dare not—It is a dream! And the anxious, fearful questioning, Do you see, Adam? Can you see it?

He said, I see it, and she cried out and said, I truly thought I slept and dreamed it.

It was a day and a night before they reached the river bank, stumbling down through green grass under the shade of leaves: a land of trees and fruit and running water; of birds and beasts and cattle—chazir and b'hemah, s'gala and

zarifah, the same tracks there by the margin of the shallows
—they ran headlong down to plunge themselves in, clothed
as they were; so that afterwards they stripped the deerskins
off to dry, and lay naked beside the river in the sun.

—It is the same as the garden, Eve said.

There were leopard tracks there down to the water's edge,
also. Adam noticed them, and leaning nearer, forgot them
again, watching the woman as she lay, one slim arm flung
over her eyes against the sun, and she said, It is just as the
garden was before: the same.

And then, seeing the man's eyes on her, she stretched out
her left hand to feel the deerskin, if it was dry; turning and
pulling it over to cover herself.

They went no farther that day; nor the next. Because
there was fruit to hand, and the river water to drink, and a
little of the corn remained, they rested there easily three days
until the Sabbath again, until the weariness of the long journey
was past.

For a time they were content to remain there, wanting no
more than this: to swim a little, wander a little way for the
nearer fruit; not far; to lie on the river bank naked for the
pleasure of the sun, half naked in the sleepy warmth of it;
to fall asleep easily in some warm hollow bedded down safe
under the rushes there, and to sleep dreamless, and to forget.
In the day's sun lying between sleeping and waking they
talked together often of this new land and what they would
do here; how they would make a new shelter taller and more
spacious than the last, how they would till the ground.
They talked, but not often, of their flight from the garden,
and the way of it; wondering at the words which the Lord
God had said to Igwana before, saying that the woman would
bruise his head; and to the woman, that she should bring

forth children in sorrow; watching the river go by and wondering at these things, but not often. And sometimes, seeing their two heads there in the river side by side, the dark and the fair, the same and not the same, they studied the little creases that came by wondering and frowning where the brow had been smooth as still water.

But of the one thing that stood at the gate of their minds, to trouble them, they spoke not at all.

With the resting, their strength returned, and with it a certain restlessness.

Adam, lifting his eyes to look about him, shaded his eyes to survey the farther hills for the first time, and the untrodden forests; watching the far flight of some bird high over them against the sky, a dark speck against the blue; and the thing broke through and flooded his soul with despair, because the woman said it is just as the garden, the same: and it was not the same.

He thought she looked at the hills, but she was watching him secretly, half smiling as she stood, and then not smiling at all; and she turned away walking, the skirt of her deerskin against her thighs and her hair unbound. She had slit the deerskin, in the long hours by the river, and sewn it again, not with lianas but with thongs cut from the hide itself, drawing it close to her skin. The sun made a sheen on her bare arms and legs, the colour of honey against the brown; her hair like the ripe corn nodding as she walked. She was walking down towards the river rushes and turned her head to look back at him, so that he went down after her.

He lay with her then: not there on the open bank under the sun but a little way apart, under the darkened shade with the rushes close and secret about them, hidden; not as he had lain with her beside the thán, dragonfly and kingfisher and the fragrance of the grasses, but now plunged in sweet torment beyond the world of these things, loosening the thongs to know her naked face to face, one flesh belovèd; and it was as if in the flight of their twin souls locked together, somewhere beyond the whispered cries of his worshipping her, his name on her lips, he might lose himself out of memory altogether, where the remembrance and the heartache of it all could no more reach him, winged in spirit; and in the flesh find refuge in a death of sleep at last.

They made a shelter of leaves there over against the river as before, and tilled the ground as they tilled it in the garden, sowing the little seed that remained in their pouches, and some they found growing wild beside the river again; they gathered fruit from the trees to eat, and honey, and berries and the white herb root, and deadwood for their fire at evening, enclosing the place with hedges as Adam had enclosed the adamah: and Eve said, It is the same as the garden; but it was not.

In the track of the leopard they found blood and bones, of what creature they could not tell, so little remained; and Adam made a stake to arm himself and tipped it with flint as a fang or a claw, which he carried always in his hand when he went outside the hedges and into the forest.

Through the long days that followed they watched the corn each morning a little higher, and the green stems rising among it which were not corn, nor planted by Adam: thorns and briars to be torn down with hands and hewn out, the strangling weeds to be uprooted one by one, with aching backs under the sun, day after day. At first they worked together and then afterwards, when the woman grew heavy with child, Adam laboured alone. Six days out of the seven he worked through all the hours of daylight, morning to dusk; but for the abundance of weeds and for want of rain half the crop failed before it was grown, and it was as if he worked to no purpose. When Eve spoke to him, he answered bitterly. Pray to the Lord God, she told him: call on Elohim as you called before, why don't you, Adam? It may be he will send us rain . . .

And he said, What is the use. How will he hear us in this place? Or if he heard us, do you think he would answer us?—seeing what we have done.

But he prayed to the Lord God nevertheless, lifting his face to heaven in the cool of the day, in the first stirring of evening, with the breath of the gentle wind on his cheek. And it was true, as Eve said, that the presence of Elohim was in this place also.

—Surely the Lord God will not be angry with us forever, she said. And shall he who made us cast off utterly?

So Adam lifted his face to heaven, and because the Lord God had said, I will not forsake you, he was sure; and because the Lord God had said, If you keep my commandments, he was afraid; but he prayed nevertheless, and it rained all through that night until the morning, a gentle rain, so that the remainder of the crop was saved for the harvest.

He fetched fruit and corn meal for her within the shelter where she lay, and brought water from the river to cool her face, soothing her fretfulness with helpless patience; marvelling at the thought of the new life beating there under the brown deerskin which covered her, moving, stirring, she told him and he felt it for himself. He set his palm gently there, smiling when she smiled, wondering what manner of creature this would be, which the Lord God had given them; thinking of the doe with young, and the lamb of the sheep; remembering the cub of ch'horiyah, how it had played between his feet, the young lion. Eve's hand covered his own, and he looked up again to the pale blue of her eyes under their lashes, her hair as honey when it is gathered new; her hair braided back smoothly from the pallor of her face, and her eyes smiling with a new tenderness; and he was afraid for her.

While she slept he wandered a little way; but not far; restless with the dark mood of bitterness upon him because he loved her, and was afraid for her; and it was not as the garden had been, and he knew it never would be the same. Though it was true that the presence of the Lord God was here, yet his voice could no longer be heard walking in the cool of the day; he no longer spoke with them, as he had spoken in the former days. And though it was true that Adam had prayed for rain, and it had rained all through the night; yet whether the rain was from the Lord God, or whether it rained of itself, who could tell?

And it was as if the voice of Igwana was soft by his ear again, to whisper it, Who can tell?

He saw in imagination the garden again as he remembered it—as he would always remember it: the brown slope of the adamah jewelled with the dew upon it, and the morning sun over the forest; the riverfalls and the hanging willows, the grassglades and hairferns and the purple fruit clusters; the saplings and cedars and the little leaves that stood against the sun: the bird that stood on his hand and the bush-tail leaping, and every creature.

And standing there by the river, near by the shelter to hear if Eve should call him, he knew that he might find all these things again, if he looked for them, in the land where he was. And he knew that the presence of the Lord God was with him always; and that if somehow he could trust him again, and not doubt, he might ask what he would, and Elohim would hear him. And he lifted his face then, and prayed for Eve, that it might be well with her; until the dark mood was lifted from him with faith, and in the gathering darkness he smiled, thinking of the young lion, how the woman had held it warm against her breast.

And of all the scenes of the garden remembered, only one remained to trouble him, there by the river; which had stood at the gate of his mind from the day of his disobedience, and would remain with him all the days of his life, and with his seed forever: somewhere between the adamah and the thán the man and the woman walking hand in hand, naked and unashamed: Adam and Ishah as they had been, and might have been always, and were no more.

Author's Note

SPEECHES for Adam, Igwana and the woman, where not taken from the Genesis account, are freely invented. The words ascribed to the Lord God are taken generally from scripture, though not always from Genesis, and not necessarily verbatim. Occasionally, for the sake of continuity or clarification, there are exceptions to this rule, the more important being noted below. But I have taken this liberty very seldom.

In order to avoid the impression that Adam, in, for example, naming the animals, spoke English, I have now and then introduced proper names, sometimes from the Hebrew, or—since there is no reason to suppose that Adam spoke Hebrew either—derived from Eastern languages; sometimes my own invention entirely. From the Book of Job I have taken Behemoth, Leviathan and the unicorn, and the names of certain stars. The two accounts of the creation of man given in, respectively, the first and second chapters of Genesis, I have assumed to refer to one and the same event.

Although the reconstruction of the garden of Eden given here is largely imaginary, it is written entirely within the framework of Genesis 2:4—4:1. No material detail of the Bible narrative has been omitted, and it has been my intention throughout to add nothing which is at any point contrary to it.

While grateful for a great number of commentaries read, I am chiefly indebted to *The Nature and Destiny of Man* by Reinhold Niebuhr (Charles Scribner's Sons), *An Old Testament Commentary for English Readers*, edited by Charles John

Ellicott, D.D. (Cassell and Company), and the *Analytical Concordance of the Bible* by Robert Young, LL.D (The Religious Tract Society).

The specific creation of man by God in his own image involves factors unknown to biology, incredible to materialism and impossible to atheism. It is not surprising, therefore, that the theory of the evolution of man from an ape-like creature should have gained widespread acceptance as a scientifically attested fact, which it is not, rather than a logical deduction with circumstantial evidence in its support, which it is. Nevertheless, whether considered as historical fact, allegorical truth, myth or legend, the story of Adam remains the story of Everyman. Other accounts may explain the origin and physical stature of modern man; we have yet to find an alternative to the Fall to account for his nature.

Notes on the Text

Page

1. *The Dragon:* Cf. Rev. 12:9; 20:2. The Genesis word 'serpent' (Heb. *nachash*) is used elsewhere to describe Leviathan (Isa. 27:1), and clearly cannot be confined to the literal meaning here, prior to the curse.

15. *the adam:* Heb. *Adam,* may be taken as a proper name, or as simply 'the man.' It is frequently used in the O.T. in the sense of 'mankind' (e.g. 'Man is born to trouble, as the sparks fly upward').

16. *Elohim:* Heb. 'God' ('Lord').
    'hovah-Elohim (or *Jehovah-Elohim*)*:* Heb. 'The Lord God.' I have taken *Elohim* by itself as the more intimate term, corresponding to 'Lord,' and *Jehovah*, because of its majestic and mystic associations in scripture, as 'God'; but strictly speaking the reverse is correct.

28. *re'em:* Heb. 'unicorn.' The animal is named in Job. 39:9 and elsewhere; but *re'em* is often held to refer to the rhinoceros.

31. *levi-i-g'wána:* an invented name, though the approximation to 'iguana' is deliberate.

33. *Adamah:* Heb. 'tilled land,' derived from *adam.*

34. *Behemoth:* 'large beast,' as the Hebrew plural (of dignity) of *b'hemah,* 'beast' or 'cattle.' It is uncertain whether it is the elephant or hippopotamus, but from the description given in Job 40:15 I have preferred the former. Alternatively, some now extinct animal.

35. *To keep the ground:* the word 'keep' suggests from some danger.

Page

39. *Leviathan:* Heb. 'water monster,' the crocodile. The word is found in Job 41, though the etymology is not, *thán* being invented.

57. *The Woman:* Gen. 2:22, 'the Lord God ... made ... a woman, and brought her unto the man,' implies that she was not made on the spot, nor in a moment. The Hebrew is literally *built he up into a woman*, with both time and care.

58. *the back of God:* Cf. Exod. 33:23. Moses saw the 'back parts' of God. The description here is scriptural.

60. *from your side:* not necessarily 'rib' in the Hebrew.

61. *—at last!* The sense is implied in the Hebrew.
    Ish ... Ishah: Heb. 'man,' 'woman' (*womb-man* is quite possibly the English, similar derivation).
    Ishah, the woman: The speech that follows in the Genesis account (2:24), 'Therefore shall a man leave his father and his mother ...' is evidently spoken by the Lord God in commentary (Cf. Matt. 19:4), and I have omitted it as being unintelligible to Adam at this point.

85. *Abir:* Heb. 'angel' or 'messenger.'

90. *as the angels:* Heb. *Elohim*. The word is plural, 'gods,' or could be the plural of dignity (as elsewhere, with a singular verb), 'God.' Only once in the Bible is it translated 'the angels,' namely in Psalm 8, 'For thou hast made him a little lower than the angels': but in so much the same context that I have adopted it, as more appropriate to the sense of the words 'the man is become as one of us,' later on (Gen. 3:22).

119. *in the flesh with sorrow:* The words do not occur in the Bible. I have added them in order to clarify the reason for the expulsion, as it is generally accepted by expositors.

122. *Elohim would have given us the fruit:* Cf. Rev. 2:7, 'To him that overcometh will I give to eat of the tree of life, which is in the midst of the paradise of God.'

Notes on the Text

Page

123. *My eve:* The Hebrew word, romanized, is *(c)havvah*, or *Eva*, 'life'; but I have retained the more familiar form.

130. *Wings:* of the cherubim. Cf. Ezek. 10:5.

134. *lay with her:* The Genesis account reads 'knew' (Eve his wife) just as, after the Fall, they knew they were naked, which does not mean they had not been naked previously.